FAMILY VALUES

MATTHEW LEDREW

FAMILY VALUES

THE XANDER DREW SERIES

Published in Canada by Engen Books, St. John's, NL.

Library and Archives Canada Cataloguing in Publication

LeDrew, Matthew, 1984-, author
      Family values / Matthew LeDrew.

(The Xander Drew series ; 4)
ISBN 978-1-926903-93-4 (softcover)

      I. Title. II. Series: LeDrew, Matthew, 1984- . Xander
Drew series ; 4.

PS8623.E424F34 2018   C813'.6   C2018-906315-7

Copyright © 2018 Matthew LeDrew

NO PART OF THIS BOOK MAY BE REPRODUCED OR TRANSMITTED IN ANY FORM OR BY ANY MEANS, ELECTRONIC OR MECHANICAL, INCLUDING PHOTOCOPYING AND RECORDING, OR BY ANY INFORMATION STORAGE OR RETRIEVAL SYSTEM WITHOUT WRITTEN PERMISSION FROM THE AUTHOR, EXCEPT FOR BRIEF PASSAGES QUOTED IN A REVIEW.

This book is a work of fiction. Names, characters, places and incidents are products of the author's imagination or are used fictitiously. Any resemblance to actual events or locales or persons living or dead is entirely coincidental.

Distributed by:
Engen Books
www.engenbooks.com
submissions@engenbooks.com

First mass market paperback printing: December 2018

Cover Image: Matthew LeDrew

For
Ellen

PROLOGUE

Los Angeles,
California

"Is that the best you can do?" Rae Stevens said, yelling into his cell phone as the reception cut in and out. Somewhere in the back of his mind he knew that speaking louder would not make the signal any clearer, but in the moment he could not stop himself from doing so every time.

Rae was an investment banker, one of very, *very* few to have come out the better for the housing market crash. In the months leading up to the crash he'd had a strange inkling, a sort of benign intuition. It came to him every morning as he was drinking his coffee and staring blankly at the morning news. It was the desire for a cigarette long after he'd quit smoking, just a nagging thought that came from nowhere and went nowhere but wouldn't go away: the thought that he should short the market. That was a bad idea by any measurable metric, he knew, and yet the idea persisted so much that he started funneling small amounts from each paycheck into the idea. He kept it secret and hid it from everyone else that worked at Shane International. If anyone found out that he was trying to short the market, in that economy, he would have been laughed out of the office. He'd have never worked anywhere in this city again.

But against all odds the market *had* crashed, and he was left on that black day with a short of just north of the low seven-figures. He hadn't been sure, but he didn't think he'd been the only one to have made the call: while Shane lost out – everyone did – they weren't hit nearly as hard as the other businesses. In the years since, Rae had often wanted to get a look at the books from that time and see just how much Shane had shorted.

He bumped shoulders with a man walking the opposite way as him down the sidewalk. He stopped to apologize, but the man had already gone on, lost in the crowd of people that made their way through the evening rush hour of human traffic. The sidewalks were wide but it never seemed to matter: there seemed to be no limit to the people. They crowded and packed themselves in, moving in unison at a lock-stepped pace until someone slowed down to look at something or tie their shoe and the whole block became bottle-necked. Human traffic could be worse than vehicular traffic, because at least vehicles had brake lights. Humans just ground to a halt divorced from the misery they caused behind them as the person following them struggled not to fall over while they avoided them, and the person behind that, and the person behind that.

"Get me Tyler Carter on this phone, right now," Rae said through gritted teeth, trying and failing to stop his tone from crossing the line from assertive into aggressive.

"I don't rightly care if he's in a meeting. Get him *out* of the meeting, get him *onto* the phone, and get him to explain to me what his branch is doing spending the last eight months digging through financial records for the entire west coast." He stopped at a hot dog vendor and the traffic behind him diverted, as if they'd known ahead of time that he was going to do so. He gestured to the specific dog he wanted, one that was just a little overdone, and then to the style of bun he wanted (whole wheat). The vendor, a man in his twenties with dark skin who had clearly gotten so sick of his hairnet that he simply shaved all the hair from his head, raised the bun with a pair of tongs and pointed to the grill. Raw shook his head, and the vendor put the dog in the bun, untoasted.

"He's on with Craig? Fine, get Craig on the line too. We can three-way the call like they did Tyler's wife." He handed the vendor a bill, took his hot dog and smeared a dollop of spicy mustard on it, then turned and merged back into the torrent of pedestrian traffic that made its way down Nordoff Street. "I don't give a fuck if you don't care for my language," he said between bites of his hotdog, the fluffy bread muffling the sound of his voice. "His branch has been liquidating assets like it's the goddamn Purge, so when he agrees to speak with me and let me know why, I'll watch my language; until then I couldn't give a good god damn."

The hotdog was gone in three bites. He ran the napkin across his mouth roughly, then shoved it into his pocket.

The street was hot. The streets were always hot in Los Angeles, bathed with the sun's rays all day until they were like lava. He could feel it even through the thick rubber soles of his shoes, the heat energy radiating up through him like a battery with every step he took. Every part of him was warm from the sun: his dark hair trapped heat and seemed to keep it on his head like an oven, as did his suit. There had been a time when he would have said you were crazy if you'd told him that he would have gotten used to the heat, and even enjoyed it, and yet here he was: choosing to make his call to Tyler Carter's branch over the phone rather than from his office.

The perceived lack of privacy of the street did not bother him. In truth, the street was more private than his office. His office was filled with people with a vested interest in what he was saying: competitors vying to outdo and out-scoop him, employees wondering about the security of their positions, and people just interested in the office gossip of Rae Stevens getting on the phone with a branch manager and calling them out. The street however was filled with people stuck in their own worlds and their own conversations: it was packed tight with people who had programmed themselves to ignore, not people programmed to listen. People on the street in the middle of their commutes walled themselves off with bubbles, their eyes buried in their phones or the people in front of them or the constant barrage of advertisements that whizzed by on every available surface.

There was a muffled sound on the other end of the line, with the sort of pace and continence that only came with speech. It had the tonality of the adults from the old Peanuts cartoons, accompanied by the staccato rustle of clothes.

Rae stopped in mid stride, and the woman walking

behind him had to pivot mid-stride to stop from colliding with him. His face was growing flush. It did this when he was angry but couldn't vent said anger. It didn't form in perfect round circles on his cheeks like in the cartoons: his rage flush came in in splotchy hive-like patches with the loose borders of eastern-European countries.

"Was that Tyler?" he barked into the phone when the person he had been speaking to returned. "Did you just put the phone down to talk to Tyler right then?" He started to walk again. He had only paused while unable to vent himself, as though the act of holding in the rage had ceased all other bodily functions.

Someone pushed their way past him, nudging the arc of their shoulder into the blade of his. They went by without stopping, disappearing into the crowd in front of Rae before he got even a cursory glance.

"Fucker!" Rae yelled. "No, not you, Jeff." He paused. "Actually, scratch that, *definitely* you, Jeff. Fuck you, fuck Tyler Carter, and fuck the entire San Diego branch. If you know something, you are *required* to tell me. I require it. Me. Well I don't much give a shit if you don't think I can require it of you, I am."

He looked at his phone, which was flashing red. "Fucker hung up on me."

His shoulder ached where he'd been tapped. He rubbed it briefly as he passed by a vendor that had set up selling water from a bin, then pressed redial on his phone. It went to voicemail.

"Fuck."

There was a homeless woman sitting in the street near him with a jar for donations. She didn't make eye contact or show interest in receiving them, even at this hour. The flood of traffic parted to give her a wide berth, transients parting to flow around her and then remerge once past, like a river parting around an obstructing stone. Rae regarded her for a moment, then stepped to one side to the side of the street to run through his contacts.

His shoulder stung, the sort of sudden throb that comes with a cramp and lingers. He brought his hand to it again, pressing the chubby flesh of his fingers into the chuck. The sting intensified and he hissed through clenched teeth.

When he pulled his hand away there was blood on it, his pointer and middle fingers coated.

"Fuck?" he said under his breath, reaching back around to his shoulder and feeling for the source of the velvet redness. He rummaged until his fingers found a scant hole in his blazer, wriggling their way inside until eventually finding the stinging fresh orifice. It resisted his prodding, sending out blazing white shards of pain through his nervous system.

"Fuck!" he exclaimed, no longer a question but a definitive statement.

People were cascading around him now, as they had the homeless woman a moment ago. They parted about five feet in front of him as he pushed out from the wall, pulling at the fabric of his shirt to try and get a look at the hole he couldn't possibly get, a dog chasing its tail. They parted past as more and more blood seeped into the dark blue of his blazer. He tried to stop several people, but they each kept their eyes locked on the street in front of them or on their screens or on the next crosswalk signal.

"Hey," he said, reaching out to one young pedestrian, who pulled away briskly. He wasn't even sure if the young woman had noticed him or not, or if she had just avoided him via some sort of sixth sense. If she had noticed him, she hadn't paid him any mind. She, along with all the others, moved freely about him.

Someone pushed into him again, this time coming at him head-on. He hadn't seen it coming until it was too late and they had connected full force, pushing their shoulder and torso into his collarbone and gut the way his high school football coach had taught him years ago. It was enough force to push him to the ground, and he landed against the sidewalk with an impact that rocketed up through his tailbone and out through the back of his head. He made a guttural sound as his head rocked back, and this time he saw the person who had hit him: it was a man. A young man, by the looks of things, though he only saw the back of his head. He had brown hair that was neither long nor short, but that in-between length favored by boy bands and independent authors. There was scruff running down his jawline, sprawling out in all directions. He was wearing a jacket that was very, very dark blue – possibly even black.

"Hey!" Rae tried to shout, but his voice caught in his throat. There was pain emanating from his collarbone where he'd been struck, and even the act of exercising the connecting tissue of his larynx caused it strain. He balked, reaching his hand up to his throat and smearing the blood on it, making a subtle red ring there.

Tension pooled into the center of his chest and clung there, weighing down his lungs and making it hard to breathe. He coughed once, and then again, and his mouth filled with the iron bile of stomach acid. He groaned as still more people shifted past him, one coming close enough to nearly step on his hand. He forced himself to turn over and placed both palms flat against the sidewalk to prop himself up.

The second he tried to rise he felt a ripping, grating pain in his abdomen. He peered down and there was blood again, but it wasn't hadn't crossed from his shoulder, there was a new patch growing slowly from his side.

"Fuck," he said again, as loud as he could but still breathy. The red blotch was the shape of Texas, and grew the more he tried to move. He winced, tried to push himself up into a position he could rise from, then fell again.

"Need a hand?" came a voice from above Rae, what seemed like an eternity later. He turned his eyes up and someone was standing over him, his face silhouetted by the harsh LA sun.

"Thank you," Rae said hoarsely, raising his arm. The young man took it and brought him to his knees with considerable strength, grabbing him under the opposite armpit and helping him to rest against the sheer glass wall of the Coldwell building closest to them. "Thank you," he said again, when he felt his body shift into a restful position for the first time in what felt like eons. He rested his hand on the swell of his gut, covering the ever-expanding edges of the red stain there.

The young man nodded, looking from one side of the street to the other.

"My phone," Rae said, motioning to his breast pocket. "Do you have a phone? Call for help."

"I have a phone," the Samaritan said, though he made no motion to reach for one.

People were passing by the both of them now in a wide favor, the median distance seeming to have widened by half now that there were two of them.

The sun beat down oppressively, falling on the dark blue jacket Rae's helper was wearing. It must have been uncomfortably warm, but he didn't take it off, even to use it to cushion Rae. Instead he let sweat bead along the ridge of his brow and trickle down his face, tumbling through the maze of scruffy, wiring hair that lined the ridge of his jaw.

Rae's breath caught in his throat, and as it did, his helper leaned forward, taking him by the shoulder and pressing them both together.

Pain belched up through Rae's torso in ways he'd never thought possible before, coming in waves and pulling and tearing and pushing all at the same time. He felt tension in his gut loosen as he voided bowel and bladder, the pain suddenly replaced with a sticky warmness that started at his neck and pushed its way down.

The young man still looked from side to side, not acknowledging the small sounds escaping Rae as he pulled them together again, then again, then again. Each time he shifted slightly, but only slightly, and Rae could see the handle of the blade the young man held, but not the rest of it. The handle terminated at Rae's midsection, and he didn't have the prescience of mind to understand where the thin metal had gone or why this young man would be holding a handle with nothing attached to it.

The man dressed in blue pulled them together one last

time, closer than he had any time before, moving the embrace from a quick clasp between friends to the sort of intimate grasping of lovers in the cool of an autumn night. When Rae looked, even the handle was gone now.

Finally the youth turned and looked at him, just as his vision was tunneling around the edges, the darkness closing in like the end of an old-timey black and white film. Rae's young assailant turned to him and locked eyes with him, and Rae saw that they were light blue… the type of blue that only seemed to exist in movies, almost the same clear white as the surrounding sclera. As the darkness pushed itself in to tiny pinpricks and then winked out, they maintained eye contact to the last, with the young man's rough-hewn face was as stony and ridged as a seasonal poker player.

When not even the bright light of California could make it through the dark that engulfed Rae, the young man withdrew his hand, sans blade, covered in dark, silky redness. He paused and watched Rae's unmoving, un-breathing form for a time, absorbing the weight of him. After watching the flow of traffic for some time, the youth took off his jacket and draped in over Rae, hiding the expanding emerging blood. He looked back over his shoulder, waiting for a break in the stream of pedestrians, then grabbed the felt hat that had been resting next to the homeless woman. She did not notice. He propped it next to Rae, stood, and then was part of the crowd as if he'd never been there.

After twenty minutes of nearly constant rush hour traffic, someone finally dropped a dollar in Rae's hat.

Luka sat on the edge on his bed as all around him, children slept.

His room wasn't his room. By rights, it shouldn't have even been called a room -- people called them rooms to imbue a sense of normalcy that wasn't present otherwise. In truth they were wards: large rooms with lines of beds, arranged geometrically and bolted to the floor. Each was evenly spaced from the next, almost exactly one half-bed apart from the next. They were in two rows of ten beds each, the room long and narrow and claustrophobic. The door was slender and tall, and looked like something out of a Tim Burton movie, but the entire opposing wall was one bay window that continued into the next ward, from when the two spaces had been one.

It was an orphanage. They didn't call them orphanages anymore though; they called them Residential Care Facilities or Short-Term Care Facilities or Long-Term Care Facilities, but a place didn't change just because you change the name. It was the same building it had been when the Catholics had owned it, as it had been when the government owned it, and as it was now that LA Sun Children owned it. It could change owners and names and terms a thousand times and still be the only thing it could be: a shadow at high noon, not seen but also not forgotten, the darkness just under your feet.

Luka was fourteen. He'd come to LA Sun after his mother had been pulled over on a DUI driving him home from school on Monday. He'd been told, repeatedly, that he'd likely only be there for a night, until mid-day at the most. Just long enough for a hearing and a date and a screening, and back his mom would be. He hadn't seen his father since he was seven and he had no other relatives, so that night-at-most was spent in the small narrow room with the tall slender door at LA Sun.

While she was being processed, the officers had found an old syringe in Luka's mother's purse, and she'd been charged with a felony and booked. Monday night had come and gone, then Tuesday, then Wednesday, and now in the middle of Thursday night Luka wondered if the remainder of his four years until age of majority would be spent in a ward that was called a room with twenty other children, designed by an architect to fit as many children in it as legally allowed.

He'd been sitting on the edge of his bed for almost two hours, listening to the uneven rhythm of all the other children's restful sleep. There was harsh orange light coming it from the window illuminating every square inch of the room, the castoff from a takeaway chicken neon sign across the road. His eyes could not get used to it. Something about the specific colour never felt right, never felt natural.

The food was not what he was used to, more greens and starch than he was used to having in his diet. He had had painful gas since nine the first night, and it didn't show any sign of letting up.

There was a boy next to him with a large black bruise covering the left side of his face. His lips were swollen and his eye bulged from its socket, fighting the confines of its closed lid. Luka found himself staring at him over and over again, having to remind himself to stop near-constantly. The boy was no more than twelve, but Luka thought he was closer to ten.

He wondered where his mother was, if they had rooms with lots of beds like this wherever she was.

There was a shadow at the door, suddenly, and Luka turned.

The shadow was tall, almost the full height of the tall, slender doorway. It made the person the shadow belonged to look stretched out, a demonic long-legged spider that had spun its way down from a higher ring of hell to visit Luka in his bed.

"Luka," the shadow said, in a hushed whisper. Luka froze. He went so ridged that he thought the blood in his veins had gone still as well. "Luka," the shadow said again.

Despite his own best interests and best judgement, Luka felt his feet touch the floor. Endorphins rushed through him, telling him both to run and to investigate at the same time, and although his brain was telling him to do the former, he watched himself, as if from outside his own body, doing the latter.

The shadow squat down as Luka got closer, suddenly lower than eye level with him. It did not halt Luka's growing sense of unease, nor did it stop him from eliminating the distance between them. "It's time to get out of here, Luka," the shadow said. Its voice was raspy and androgynous, neither harsh nor welcoming. The person squatting in the doorway seemed to exist in the space between all things, perfectly centered.

"My mom got out?" Luka asked, running his hand along the wisps of hair that lined his upper lip, too scant to even be called peach fuzz.

The shadow reached forward and took Luka by the arm, wrapping its slender, bony fingers completely around it. His arm looked like it had fallen into a gap in reality, simply ceasing to be and then reappearing few inches later. "I'm taking you to be with your family," the shadow person said, its smile stretching from ear to ear as it pulled Luka out of the ward with its many beds at LA Sun, and out into the harsh light of the hall.

CHAPTER ONE

The smell of the barbeque was thick on the air, making it in through the screen door and filling Tim White's home with the succulent flavour of steak.

"How's that coming?" Xander called over his shoulder, grabbing a mustard seed spice and storing it in the crook of his arm with four others he'd found. He waited for a response as he found a plate and looked for the metal tongs, but did not hear one. "Don't make them medium on the grill. You cook them rare on the grill and they rest to medium on the plate."

"Did you want to do this?" Crowley called back from her position standing over the grill, spatula in hand. "Because I don't recall you volunteering when we were handing out tasks. How about while you're in the kitchen, you get a teaspoon of mind-your-business?" She smiled, stuck out her tongue, then turned back toward the grill and shifted the cuts on it.

Xander leaned back, holding onto the island and smiled at her. When she didn't turn around again to engage him, he chuckled and shook his head, then went to the fridge and got two beers. He rested them both in his arm along with the spices and balanced his entire load precariously, stepping out to meet her just out on the back step.

Tim White lived in government-sponsored housing set in the outskirts of middle-class Los Angeles. Not that there was much of a middle-class in Los Angeles anymore, but what little there was congregated here. It was a quiet street with homes that had been designed to look designed: each one complimenting the next.

The home was only one of three on the block that was one level, the style typically called a bungalow. Tim had been injured in the line of duty as a Federal Agent, and as a result was unable to make most movements below his neck, save for some scant movement that had been saved in his left hand. He had been right handed before he was injured, something that he had come to think of as a 'cruel irony' with his best attempt at humor. As a result of his immobility, the majority of his time was spent in the main room of the house, on a bed with motorized wheels that could bring him into any room. It was easier, though, just to stay in the main room. It was a large open concept room, with a big-screen TV above a fireplace that he sometimes used for his research work.

He had insisted on remaining at work, if only in a research capacity. He'd been told repeatedly that he could and would be allowed early retirement, with commendations, but would have none of it.

His bed was now in the open space between the kitchen and the sliding glass door that led out to a back deck it was all-but impossible for him to use without an hour's preparation. He watched Xander approach, balancing the spice rubs and beverages he'd picked up, on a screen just a foot in front of him, which delivered a feed from a camera on an articulated head he controlled. Eventually Xander came into view without benefit of the camera, and there were two of them in Tim's line of sight.

"Did she sear the fat?" Tim asked as Xander stepped around him. "Tell her she has to sear the fat or it won't get that crust you want on the outside. That's why they leave the fat on the cut; you want to melt it off."

"She seared the fat," Xander said as he passed, opening the door to the porch and stepping out. He closed it behind him. As much as Tim enjoyed the fresh air, he'd discovered that if pests got in with no way for him to dispose of them, he quickly became a feeding frenzy for them. It only took one long, sleepless night of itchy red bumps he could not scratch before he decided to impose the "door stays closed" policy. Xander stepped up to Crowley, opened one of the beers, then handed it to her. She took it thankfully and took a sip, and he did the same with his own. "Did you sear the fat?" he asked, after what he felt was the appropriate hesitation. "Because you have to --"

Crowley turned, wedging the sharp metal edge of her spatula against Xander's central plexus. "You can totally cook them if you want. I'm cool with it."

Xander raised his arms and stepped away, smiling.

Lisa sat under an umbrella nearly, bathed in a protective bubble of shade. She looked up from her book and tilted up her sunglasses, displacing several locks of her curly sun-kissed blonde hair. "She will stab you with that, you know," she said dryly, eyeing Xander as he backed away.

Crowley turned her head slightly and stuck out her tongue again.

Xander smiled. "Reading?"

She held up the book, which had a bright yellow starburst in the center of its covered, surrounded by the smooth dark blue of sky. "*The Greatest Show on Earth.*"

Xander raised an eyebrow at her.

"What? I have layers."

He smirked.

"I can have layers!" She let the book flop down onto her stomach in mock-exasperation. It rested there on the swell of her stomach which had only recently begun to show signs of distorting her figure. She kept her feet up, and kept herself out of the harsh Los Angeles sun.

Xander smiled, shrugged, and took a sip of his beer as he stepped back into the house, closing the door behind him. It was warm inside, the house furnished with an orangey wood colour and smooth floors that were both stylish and easier for Tim's mobility. They absorbed light though, and the inside of the house was cooler and darker than the outside. With the two of them inside looking out at the woman outside in the bright sunshine of life, it was like they were looking out into a different world. Crowley was wearing jean shorts and a shirt that was too big for her that she let drape down over one shoulder. Xander caught his gaze lingering on her briefly as he shut the door, before he turned away.

When he turned away from the light of outside, his smile faded almost instantly.

Tim watched him approach and narrowed his eyes at him as he did. "Did she sear the fat?"

"Probably not," Xander replied curtly, taking a folding chair off the wall next to Tim and sitting on it. "Do you have anything?"

Tim's expression, as little as he found he could differentiate between them of late, became taut and serious. He closed the tab he was on with some quick motions of his fingers, and opened another. The window was filled with smaller squares that looked like sticky-notes, and as he hovered over each one, they expanded. "There was an ATM heist on Stine. By which I mean, they took the ATM. Pulled it out of the ground with a chain."

There was a black and white security video on the screen when he moused over it, from a high angle. There was a truck attached to the electronic teller with a thick chain, and after three attempts, it came loose of its foundation and skidded down the street after the truck, sending sparks in all directions until it was out of the camera's view.

"No," Xander said, shaking his head imperceptivity. "He wouldn't do a money-grab like that."

"He could recoup some of the losses you got from his bank..."

"In all the time I've been following him, he's never gone after money. He's gone after *things* that have *gotten* him money, but never the money itself. There's always a step between him and the money, a process, a sale."

Tim nodded, then moved on to the next icon. "There was a pharmacy scam in West Odindale; apparently one of the pharmacists was short-changing people their oxycontin and sending it out the back door on the sly. Some-one got wind and tried to knock it over on stash day, one person died. The dirty pharm is in custody now."

"Flag it," Xander snapped, taking a drink from his beer.

"There have been three murders in the business district, not far from the bank you dealt with. Last one was in broad daylight on Nordoff Street, right in the middle of rush-hour."

"Anything in common?"

"They all worked for Shane International, but a lot of people work for Shane. And these were weeks apart. But, still." Tim bobbed his eyes in a way that Xander had come to recognize as meaning he was tilting his head. Tim was still doing those motions, and in his mind's eye they were still happening, they just weren't translating into action.

There was laughter from outside, and Xander turned back to see that Lisa had laid her book on the table and was now holding a plate out for Crowley to place the steaming meat onto. Steam and smoke bathed them both, surrounding them in wispy clouds that caught the sun's rays and trapped them. They danced across Crowley's shoulders and got into her hair, which was drawn up in a bun and had only just shyly started to streak blonde from the summer shine.

"Ignore it," Xander said finally, keeping his eyes on the girls as they came toward the sliding door. His voice was rushed and impatient.

Tim's eyebrows rose. "Three dead."

Xander turned and glared at him. "Three is the problem. There's not one person on Nordoff Street or anywhere in the business district that would cross Stephen Fields. Not for a stick of gum, not to fuck a model, not for a million dollars. And if one ever did, that one would be made an example of and there would never be another. Three? Three is a statistical impossibility with Fields, especially when there are more than enough people that *are* willing to play ball with him."

Tim's eyebrows remained raised.

"It's not him. Ignore it."

Tim tisked, then moved on to the next file as Crowley and Lisa entered through the sliding glass door and brought the steaks over to the island in the kitchen. The plate was steaming hot and the steaks looked juicy and plump, a thin layer of peppercorn just touching their ridges.

"The, ah," Tim lowered his voice slightly. "There have been some missing children."

At the table, Lisa's head turned slightly.

Xander watched as Tim hovered over the file, and school photos began to display one after another, each fading into the next like a slideshow.

"It's hard to say how many, they're all in the system. It'd be hard to say it wasn't at least five in the last month and a half."

"Is that uncommon?" Xander asked. His gaze had shifted from the screen to Lisa, who was still back onto them. He could see the swell of her belly better from this angle, and the way it just made her shirt ride up slightly, showing the pale skin of her midriff.

"Sadly not particularly, but the MO on these five are… similar. Middle of the night, no signs of struggle, nothing suspicious in the backgrounds of the workers... There's something there."

"Age?"

Tim cleared his throat, speaking quieter again. Lisa tilted her ears to compensate. "Between nine and fifteen," he said, as low as her could.

Lisa dropped one of the steak-knives onto the plate they were setting.

"You told me once that you came at Fields through his work in the sex trade?" Tim asked Xander, allowing his voice to return to its normal cadence.

Xander nodded. He'd met the crime boss named Stephen Fields just after coming to Los Angeles, in time to witness him murder a young boy who had witnessed Fields' men gunning down his mother. Since then he'd been trying to dismantle as much of Fields' criminal organization as he could: he destroyed the funds in a bank Fields owned, worked to undermine his drug operations in several schools, and – saliently – had burned one of Fields' brothels to the ground and made sure many of the young women who'd been working there got back to their families. "You think he's recouping his workforce?"

Tim's eyes raised again. "Do you?"

There was a long pause then. Xander looked from Lisa to the children on the screen, and then back again. There had been a young brunette girl on the screen who looked to be thirteen, smiling brightly into the camera. It was the type of smile that to men like Fields said: 'I've never been hurt before.'

"I do," Xander said. "It's him, it's something he'd do."

Tim made a series of clicks on the icon. "It'll be on the printer when you leave."

Xander went to the kitchen table and transferred a steak from the plate in the center to one on its own. "Thank you," he smiled politely to Crowley as he took a knife and fork to it, slicing the tender meat into thin, slight pieces.

Crowley smiled back, popping a piece of her own steak in her mouth with a self-satisfied expression.

Lisa chewed slowly, still working on her first slice. She swallowed. "There was something about kids?"

Xander eyed her as he cut, then finished and made his way back to Tim's bedside. He sat on the chair, lay the plate on his lap, and stuck one of the more tender pieces on the fork, bringing it to Tim's mouth. Tim took it, with a look that said that if he could have he would have nodded respectfully at Xander.

Tim smiled. "Crowley, this is wonderful." And then to Xander: "She seared the fat."

Crowley snorted and shook her head.

"There were missing children," Xander said after a time, finally answering Lisa's question, but without addressing her directly. "Fields has them."

Without realizing she did it, Lisa brought a hand to her abdomen.

CHAPTER TWO

"We found her just like that," the chief of security said. His voice was high and he looked frail, like a scant breeze could blow him over. He had a bushy gray mustache that might have accounted for half of the weight of his head.

Duncan Taggart was crouching in an office on the twenty-fifth floor of the Shane International building, less than four feet from the body of Tilda Stine. He had the nub of a toothpick stuck in the front of his teeth and the tails of his duster were trailing the fibres of the gray industrial carpet.

Tilda Stine was in her fifties by the look of her. Her hair was gray save for the few strands of vermillion that refused to give up the ghost, and there were large circles under her eyes from many a long night spent staring at a screen. She had been a petite woman, scarcely five feet tall. She'd had a mouth full of natural, original teeth that had been kept to a pristine white shine. Duncan could see them now. She'd ended her life with her mouth hanging open, still sitting in her swivel chair.

Duncan stroked his smooth chin, sighing as he took in

Tilda's last moments. He couldn't touch her or move her or even go remotely near her, not until the medical examiner arrived. All he had was his view of her and the room, neither of which painted a particularly appealing portrait of her last moments. There were long slices down both her arms that had opened the meat underneath to the open air, the maw of them hanging open like loose punches. Her left side of her face had a long friction burn on it, and as Duncan's eyes fell across the carpet, he thought he saw the offending patch of floor that still had pieces of her face in it.

A long blade had been wedged into her just under her collarbone, pinning her back to her chair. Blood had soaked into the back cushion until it could hold no more, and was even now dribbling down the articulated leg and seeping its way into the matted gray carpet, turning it a deep black.

"She got stabbed," the security chief said, shoving his hands into his pockets.

Duncan turned slowly, peering over his shoulder. "Figured that out, did'ja? We could use a young mind like you at the Bureau." He took the toothpick out of his mouth and put it in his breast pocket, withdrawing a moment later with a cigarette which he pursed between his lips.

The chief, Cliven, considered informing him that he couldn't smoke inside the building, but thought the better of it. Instead he clasped his mouth shut, so much so that his bottom lip overextended the top by a full inch.

Duncan arose from his squatted position, stretched, and took a step back toward the door. Tilda shrunk in his field of vision, and he got more of the bay window behind her and the view of the Shane International HQ Lobby beyond that.

"Alright, you can let them in," Duncan said after a long moment, not bothering to turn around and address Cliven. He plucked the unlit cigarette back out of his mouth, its tip thoroughly moistened and flattened, and stuck it behind his ear.

Cliven walked to the office door and opened it. Two men entered, each tall and balding and trying desperately to hide that fact. Duncan recognized the first to enter as Arthur Shane, the owner of the building and company they were in. The other he didn't recognize, but he had on a purple tie. The purple tie was so tight looking that his cheeks might soon have flushed the same colour, while Shane's red tie had been undone and was hanging lackadaisically to either side of his collar.

Shane stopped when he saw Tilda, bringing his hand to his mouth and then turning away. The other man just gaped at her, his mouth as agape as the victim's.

Duncan watched the both of them react, turned and followed their lines of sight to the victim, then returned his gaze with a smirk on his face. "Shane, right?" he asked, pointing to the man in the purple tie.

Shane bristled.

The other man laughed absently, momentarily shaken out of his shock. "No, sorry. Harvey Swan, Head of the Board." He extended a hand to Duncan, who gave it one firm pump before letting it go.

"*I'm* Arthur Shane," said Arthur, pushing his arm forward.

Duncan touched it for the barest of seconds, then turned back to the body. He took the cigarette out from behind his ear and used it to point at it, then back at Shane. "Maybe then you can tell me how a woman sits like this at the desk of one of the biggest whatevers on the west coast and nobody notices for hours on end?"

Shane looked past him to Tilda. "Hours?"

Duncan raised an eyebrow at him. He turned back to Tilda, out the cigarette between his lips, then ran his fingers through his shaggy hair. "Is there security on this floor, Mr. Shane?"

"There's -"

"And don't say Cliven."

Cliven's ears got hot, and he turned and left the room.

"I need the card keys and the security tapes for this floor since hers was last used. I need to talk to any employee that walked past this office in the last eight hours. *Somebody* saw *something*. It is not conceivable that a woman can be killed in her office in a building this big and that nobody knows anything about it."

Cliven came back into the room, his face flushed of all colour. "Sir?"

"Not now," Shane and Swan said in unison, then threw each other frustrated glances that Duncan caught.

Duncan looked past them, to Cliven, whose bottom lip was once again over his top. "Spit it out, cornbread."

Cliven paused, still holding the frame of the door. "…They've found another one."

Duncan snapped his cigarette in two.

Xander sat on Tim White's back porch in the glow of an evening so windless that the discharge of the cigarette he'd finished minutes ago still hung in the air like cotton candy. The evening was still and the city was quiet here, a side of it he had yet to see since settling here.

He heard the glass door slide open behind him. He did not turn around, just took a deep breath in through his nostrils. "Crowley," he said, matter-of-factly.

She stopped, her hand still on the latch. "That's unbelievably creepy."

He hunched his shoulders, then looked back at her. She stepped up to join him at the end of the patio, staying arm's length away even when she reached the railing with him.

Tim's house bordered a walking trail, an irony Xander had chosen not to point out. As such they were far enough away from the nearest buildings that their lights shone in the still air, catching the floating wafts up from the street that twinkled in front of them and turned them bright purples and oranges and deep, deep violets.

"Lisa still upset?" he asked finally, not turning to look at her.

"Hmm? Oh. She's fine. Hormones. She's talking to Tim now about some restaurant in Jersey they both used to go to."

Xander smiled, content not to answer verbally. His nose twitched and he paused for another moment, hanging his head. "Is it too late? Should I get you two home?"

She snorted. "You met me at a club."

He smiled. "Just wondered why you came out."

She met his eye but didn't hold it. Her hair was up in a ponytail and he could see her entire face, the way her cheeks pushed up when she grinned. It was an excellent smile, in his opinion. Easily ranked in his top three, even in the short time he'd known her. "I wanted to chat with you."

"Ah, sorry. I'll come back, I just… the smoking, I know. I shouldn't."

"No, it's not… no. I wanted to chat just with you. When you were out here, without them. Not that Tim's not great, but… well. I just felt like talking to you."

He smiled again. Their hands lingered near each other on the rail of Tim's deck and he inched his closer.

She pulled hers away, bringing it up to just under her breast before forcing it back down, and he could *see* the gooseflesh shimmying its way along her arms.

"Sorry," he said, shifting his hand back. "I didn't mean… sorry. What did you want to talk about?"

She opened her mouth, closed it, then winced as she tried to think of the words. After a moment, their silence was interrupted by Tim's bellowing, earthy laughter mixing with the shrill yelps of Lisa's laughs from inside the house. They both turned to see Lisa helping Tim shift positions on the bed, and clearly some comment from one or both of them to make light of the situation had done its job.

Crowley laughed. "Did you want to go back in? Tim wanted to see if we wanted to play Pictionary on the console."

Xander pursed his lips, then nodded. He followed her halfway back to the light of the house, then stopped and let her go the rest of the way without him. He took a cigarette from his coat pocket and lit it, sending wreaths of smoke cascading around his head again.

When she reached the door, she turned back and looked at him quizzically.

"I'll be right in," he smiled, and she nodded without heart. A sullen, angry look passed over her brow and then was gone, replaced by the perfectly pleasant exterior that had been crafted over years of trial and patience.

She went back into Tim White's den and joined him and Lisa the same way she'd come, leaving Xander on the porch with his dark and wafting, stale smoke.

He took a folded sheet of paper out of his jacket and flattened it smooth, then started to read through the profiles of five missing children.

CHAPTER THREE

The Family Values Wellness Center rented a space alongside a Baptist church on Pike Avenue, in what would have been called a mother-in-law apartment back in the day. From the outside it just looked like a part of the church, the architecture making no effort to differentiate it from the rest of the building. There was a wrought iron fence around the entire structure, closing it off from the rest of Pike Avenue's steel and concrete. Inside the fence was grass, lush and green, the only grass she'd seen in the city in weeks.

Crowley stood at the gap in the fence that its entryway led from. It wasn't a gate, merely the absence of space where a gate might have been. The grounds were never closed off, which in Los Angeles meant the building managers would have to be constantly vigilant about graffiti or risk appearing derelict within a week. Her toes strode the gap between the street and the cobblestone path through greenery and into the center.

There was a smell like mineral oil on the air from a nearby spa, the sort of faint stench of ozone that produced something visceral within her, like Old Spice deodorant. She had never been able to stand the smell of deodorant, and had special disdain for any that had the image of a ship on the bottle. It didn't help that the smell had mingled with the salty starch smell of french fries deep-drying in vegetable oil from a nearby fast food pop-up, her nostrils taking that in greedily and grabbing the oxidized oil stench along with it.

She took a deep break and stepped from the concrete to the cobblestone, marking the difference in how it felt beneath her feet. The cobblestone felt spongier somehow, the soil beneath it providing more give. Tensing one final time, she opened the large orange door to Family Values.

The waiting area was conspicuously vacant. It had been sectioned off at some point in the past with a large door with reinforced glass panels between it and the remainder of the area; this was more like LA, and she felt instantly reassured that her preconceptions had not been misplaced. In truth the building was *exactly* LA, now that she saw it on the inside: the veneer of welcoming disguising the fact of guardedness.

There was a receptionist just to the other side of the glass and a buzzer just to Crowley's left, so she pushed it. The sound it made was droning, electronic white noise – she wasn't sure when it had become unfashionable to have pleasant chimes or a short tune as your indicator, but it had clearly been before this one had been installed. The sound it made was loud and ground through her. She winced as the door unlatched itself, then stepped inside.

It was warmer in this main lobby, and there was carpet. It was office-use hypo-allergenic carpet, the kind that was mostly dark blue with red and black flecks that seemed to get sent to every office in America when they opened. There were chairs but they seemed too small, like they would cease to be midway up one's back and become uncomfortable.

"What can I do for you?" came the receptionist's shrill voice. It made Crowley jump, forcing her away from the haunting rose-coloured pattern of the chair and back to reality. The voice came through the speaker just to the side of the glass she sat behind. It was very low-quality, and came out with that came metallic tinge to it that the buzzer had had.

"I, uh, I was looking to, um," she stammered, finally ending her thought as a question when she was unable to complete it as a statement, "Talk to someone?"

"Were you referred by your family doctor?"

Crowley's eyes widened slightly. "No, I'm sorr – I don't have—"

"GP?"

"I don't know what that --"

"Fill this out," the woman said without looking up, sliding several sheets of paper held together by a staple through a small opening at the bottom of the glass.

Crowley took it. The paper was crisp between her dry fingers.

The receptionist looked up after almost no time, as if surprised Crowley was still there. "Pens are on the desk," she said, motioning with her own.

Crowley turned, and sure enough there was a tiny desk between two of the horrid rose chairs, with a mug and several pens and a small stack of Highlights magazine on it. She walked over to it and sat down, picking a pen without thought and eyeing the questionnaire.

There were questions and bubbles, the sort of which she hadn't had to fill in since high-school.

She filled out her name, and below it were a list of nine questions on the first page alone. She did not fill in her real name.

Each question had five responses: Most of the Time, Often, Sometimes, Rarely, and, Almost Never. Small bubble-buttons, which she knew were called radio buttons, but still called bubble-buttons anyway. The questions were hateful to her… not so much in their phrasing, but in the way she had to answer. She kept clicking one button only to change her mind and pick another, and she wondering if that in and of itself would be a question later in the questionnaire: "Did you flip-flop on any of the previous answers? Most of Them, Often, Sometimes, Rarely, and, Almost None of Them."

I feel sad. She hovered over Often, then marked decisively in Most of the Time, before erasing it and checking Sometimes. Was it Sometimes? She had felt sad after her conversation with Xander the previous evening, but she'd had a *reason* to feel sad. Was it asking if she felt sad for no reason, or in general? Or was there no difference? Could there be people who dealt with sad things and didn't have that sadness rub off on them? That seemed unhealthy to her, like a kind of numbness. She decided it was unhealthy and that the question *meant* to ask if you feel sad for no reason, and that was only Sometimes. Or was there a reason? She supposed there was always a reason, just not one that was readily apparent. Should she choose Almost Never? Best to go middle-of-the-road, just in case.

I need to move constantly. Almost Never. There were periods, in her last apartment, when she felt like she could sit forever and just stare out the window onto the street below… or was it asking if she relocated often? It wasn't specific, but the answer was the same either way.

I feel worn out. Most of the Time. It was better than it had been months ago, but she still often felt like taffy that had been stretched too far, to the point that it could be seen through. Once in recent memory she had stood in front of a full-length mirror and lifted her shirt and been almost surprised that she couldn't see through herself.

I feel so guilty I can barely take it. Often.

When I wake up in the morning, I feel like there is nothing to look forward to. Often.

I lose track of the date and time. Most of the Time.

I think about death. Sometimes.

I get mad at myself. Often.

When something is bothering me, I cannot stop thinking about it. Often.

She looked back over her answers, and the blank radio-buttons that lined the right side of the form. In a strange way she felt guilty about her answers… it was hard to tell if she was being dramatic in them or not. She reasoned that there were likely people much worse off than she, and wondered if they would be turned down because they rushed through her because of her left-bubble answering. Maybe she should change some of the Often answers to Sometimes answers. She wished the pencil hadn't had an eraser. This would have been so much easier if it had just been one of those stubby pencils that ending in flat wood that often came with Milton Bradley games.

After scrutinizing the answer to questions three, six, and nine again, Crowley became frustrated and walked back to the receptionist and handed in the form. She took it and smiled, then perused which bubbles had been selected, and looked back to smile again, this time more forced.

"Susan has an opening for an intake interview this afternoon?" the lady said, clasping the form between thumb and forefinger in such a way that it was ridged, jutting out between them like a near-completed bridge. She said it as though it was a question, her voice rising at the end, and it was assumed that the implied question was if Crowley could come in that afternoon.

"That's fine," Crowley said, nodding emphatically. "I'd even take sooner, if there was sooner. But this afternoon is fine. It's fine. I mean, obviously, that's as soon as can be expected."

The receptionist smiled, removing the form from stabbing the air between them and placing it on the 'in' pile on her desk.

Crowley turned to leave through the annexed hall and step back into the Los Angeles sun, then stopped at the door, turned back, and sat in the unfortunate dusty-rose chair again.

CHAPTER FOUR

Lisa leaned against the glass wall of the café opposite the LA Sun Orphanage, her arms folded in front of her. She was wearing a blue blouse with short frilly arms that rippled in the scant breeze that came down the street from the west end, bringing the stench of the smog with it.

She stared across at LA Sun with an expression somewhere between curiosity and frustration. It was a similar expression that one would have when given a particularly complex mathematical equation to solve if they were not apt to it, a crease forming from her left eyebrow up into her hairline. In response, the LA Sun building stood silently across from her, monolithic and imposing and yet still in the shadow of the office buildings that surrounded it.

"Decaf, full-fat, whip," Xander said, coming out of the café and stepping up behind her. He held out a tall, paper coffee cup to her. He had his own as well, though his was much simpler: coffee, black. When he had it, he never deviated from that: coffee, black.

She turned and narrowed her eyes at him. "You don't

call it 'full fat,' you just call it 'milk.' You only need to qualify it if there's fat missing."

Xander shrugged. "I said what I said."

She glowered at him a moment longer, then took her coffee from him and had some. A truck sped by too quickly and displaced some of her blonde curls, sending them pattering against the paper walls of the cup she drank from.

Xander took a sip of his own coffee and considered lighting a cigarette, then noticed the meagre swell of Lisa's stomach and thought better of it. He fidgeted as a dull ache started in his abdomen and rippled through him, not pain exactly but disquieting discomfort. He brought his hand to his side.

Lisa noticed. "It's been doing that a lot lately."

He turned to her, surprised, but tried not to show it. "I guess."

"Since Genesis, at least."

His lip twitched at the mention of it, briefly becoming a snarl he tried to keep from her.

"Should you maybe see someone?"

He shot her a wry look.

"Well, mention it to Tim at least."

He took a sip of his coffee and turned back to the LA Sun building.

It was four stories tall but looked like far, far less. By comparison, the office building next to it was five stories tall, yet towered above it. Each floor was compressed, like old homes from the turn of the last century, and it gave a hint to the age of its design that its exterior masked. It was a concrete block of a building, with windows an equal length apart. They were long windows, and even from across the street they could see partitions in them where rooms that had formally been one had been divided into two, or in one case along the far third-floor wall, into three. There was a seascape mural along the bottom half of the first floor with colourful characters that looked to have been badly-mimicked infringements from a Pixar film, but most had been since obscured by graffiti.

Without realizing she was doing it, Lisa's free hand went to her abdomen and cradled it.

"What are we doing?" she asked, after a long moment of silence.

Xander motioned to LA Sun with his coffee cup. He brought it back to his lips and took another long swallow. "Two main entrance points, one on the front and one on the side. Then each of the rooms on the side have fire escapes: two per floor, one per wing, except the first floor. Not up to code; there should be a fire exit for every suite, but there isn't. But that's still six other entry exit points. Graffiti says building's in disrepair, but funding is still coming in; I checked. Disrepair is disrepair: no windows are smashed in, ergo no windows *were* smashed in, and there isn't any other sign of forced entry." He pointed to three specific places on the main floor. "Three places in the graffiti are gang markers, crossed out and another replacing it, then again, then back to the first. This is disputed territory, makes sense, we're on the wall of a few different suburbs. And there's no outside play area."

He took another sip of his coffee.

Lisa looked from him to the LA Sun building, then back again. She had followed his gestures through every step he'd made: the fire escapes and the windows and the graffiti, and taken note of each of them in turn. Now she looked at them all again, noting each and making sure she recognized them for what they were, not as parts of the overall tapestry of the LA Sun building that she had mistaken them for before. That was the trick of what he did, she decided: the breakdown of something into its individual parts for scrutiny. "What does all that mean?" she asked finally, trying to tally up the results and failing to.

His mouth moved from side to side, as if it were the scales he was placing each point of data on in his mind.

Lisa watched the building as a child came to window, small with blonde hair that fell into her face.

"It means it's not Fields," Xander said finally, his voice thick with bitterness.

She turned and looked at him, so suddenly her hair whipped around and one of her curls hit her cheek.

"He wouldn't take from disputed territory. Or rather, any place he took from wouldn't be disputed. The fear that comes off this man... you'd have to see it to understand it, and I hope you never will. But this isn't him. This is something else."

"But you're going to look into it," she said, as soon as he'd finished speaking, as though she'd just been waiting for his lips to stop moving.

He turned his head slightly, his eyes travelling down from her face and seeing that her free arm still rested at her abdomen, only now the fabric of her blouse bunched slightly under the tension of her fingers. Even though it hadn't come out as a question, when his gaze found its way back to her eyes they were filled with the query of it:

waiting with tense digits for the answer.

He nodded curtly, then took another sip of his coffee.

Duncan shivered as he walked across the long corridor that divided the stairwell he'd entered from from the dark green doors of the morgue. He could hear the air conditioners running, struggling to keep the hallway cold enough that his breath could be seen each time he exhaled.

He hated the cold, recycled air that came out of the vents all around the police building. One of the few benefits to being assigned to the west coast, in his opinion, was the sun. There was nothing like California heat for his money, warmer than any place he'd ever been to except for Vegas, and without its dryness. He could feel it every time he stepped out into the sun, that warmness on his face and radiating up from his central plexus, cascading out through his veins. The second he stepped into a building though, high-pressure air-conditioners started blasting recycled Freon at him, even here in the basement of the police building, where the sun clearly couldn't reach. Even the lights seemed arranged to dissipate the heat, dim and too far apart to properly light the area, leaving gaps of black space between them. These spaces were even cooler than the rest, and he steeled himself each and every time he stepped into one, his breath flittering from his nostrils in stringy white puffs.

He yanked open the door to the morgue, hoping on some level that it would be warmer on the inside, which it wasn't.

By two tables in the center of the room was an obese man with a scruffy dark beard, and hair that came down to just touch the shoulders of his light grey scrubs. The wall behind him was lined with cabinets and more tables, each of them raised to waist height. When the man turned to greet Duncan, his whole body shifted, until the only thing that was between them was the tray of scalpels that stood at the man's crotch.

"Duncan Taggart?" the bearded man asked, with a voice that had withstood the assault of one too many Marlboroughs in its time. Duncan nodded as he entered the chilly air of the morgue, his breath barrelling out of him like steam from a train's stack as he went. The pathologist extended a gloved hand. "Travis Moore."

Duncan looked from Travis to the corpse that now lay between them, and then back again, and winced.

Travis withdrew the hand. "Right."

"Is it always this chilly down here?" Duncan asked, shuddering.

Travis nodded. "Keeps the smells down. Plus, it's a reprieve from the outside." He turned then to the first body, the one that lay between them. When he did, only his left eye shifted in its orbit to address the body, with the right remaining set on Duncan. The affect was unnerving, as though half of the man's face had been caught in a real-life buffering error.

Tilda Stine lay naked on the table between them, her hands settled on either side of her body in a position that Duncan had come to associate with being a corpse. Humans didn't lie like that in any other circumstance, he thought. When you slept, your arms splayed out in any and all directions, and when they put you in your coffin, they crossed your hands in front of your chest. You were only this straight, this *uniform*, on the slab.

The maw that ran through her seemed to take up the majority of her torso, and at first his body rejected his instruction to look at it, finding its way to the ample tuft of curly gray hair that puffed out of the woman's crotch.

"Tilda Stine, 43," Travis said, ignoring the swivel of Duncan's head. He had seen far worse reactions over the years.

"Damn," Duncan said, his voice croaking slightly until he found his center. "I had her pegged for mid-fifties."

One of Travis' eyes turned to regard him, the other staying firmly aimed at the red-rimmed gash bisecting Tilda. He didn't say anything, just watched as Duncan shifted uncomfortably from foot to foot. "There's smelling cream on the table, if you need."

"I'm good."

"There's no harm in --"

"I'm *good*."

Travis moved forward, closing the scant gap between his abdomen and the table. His eye shifted back toward Tilda. "The wound on the chest was made peri-mortem; it was the cause of death. Directionality shows it started from the top and worked its way down – bisecting the heart." He made a motion, as though his hand were pantomiming the blade.

Duncan shifted from foot to foot.

"I found traces in the wound, black fibres. I think it was from the chair she was on; I sent it to the lab. It implies the blade came from behind, through the chair."

"Through the chair?"

"Through the chair."

Duncan thought back to the chair Tilda had been propped up against, the type of thick leathery office chair that people got when they knew they were going to be sitting on the same device for five to ten years before the budget allowed for everyone to get new ones. "That makes no sense," he said finally, staring into the cratering maw of her torso.

"It doesn't have to make sense, it's how it is."

He frowned.

"There was bruising around the neck, peri-mortem. So if I had to guess, I'd say he grabbed her by the throat and pushed the blade through." He reached one hand around and pushed the other forward, pantomiming the action. "There's twisting to the bruising that supports that – just this slight twist where he had her in one position and pushed the blade through and she moved under his grip, slightly."

"He?"

"Hm?"

"You keep saying 'He'."

"Statistically the case."

Duncan shifted again. "You are a weird motherfucker, you know that?"

Travis gave him a dry look.

"Also, why do you keep looking at me like that? With the eye. It's creeping me out."

"It's glass."

Duncan pursed his lips, then turned to the second table. "So, the other one then?"

Travis shuffled until he was between the two tables. On the second was a large man of African descent. He was clean-shaven with only the wisps of curly gray hair poking out from around his ears. His nipples were large – so much so that Duncan had a hard time taking his eyes off of them. They stared back like the eyes of a Kraken rising out of the ocean, far lighter than the rest of his dusty brown frame.

"Whelan Davis, thirty-five. Same bruising around the neck, same blade wound through the chest."

"Okay, we done then?"

"Cause of death was asphyxiation."

Duncan stopped. He turned from Whelan, to Tilda, then back again. "Pardon?"

"He was strangled to death. The stab wound was inflicted post-mortem."

For the first time, Duncan let his gaze fall to the jagged rip of flesh that made its way from between his gargantuan nipples down to his sternum, and lingered.

After a moment, Travis began to show him the lack of blood from the wound in Whelan's chest, but by that time Duncan's mind was far away.

CHAPTER FIVE

Crowley sat at a picnic table across from the back entrance of Family Values just out of the reach of the shade that had been slowly creeping toward her since noon. The table was stained a dark brown that captured the heat of the day and held it, until she was warmed from both above and below like a grilled cheese in a hot press. She found the sun comforting, and yet with that comfort came a certain amount of disquiet: as the rays relaxed her, another part of her tensed, aware that she shouldn't *really* be relaxing. Instead of settling, her skin became sensitive to the ever-so-slight breeze, her ears keenly aware of the traffic that was just out of view beyond the borders of the yard.

She opened her eyes. There was a pigeon next to her on a nearby stone, perched as though it had some vantage point on the yard that let it see something the others did not. Its head snapped from left to right and back again over and over, its large eyes unblinking. Though its face wasn't capable of emoting, she felt as though it was stressed, somehow. There was a frenetic pace to its twitching that detonated panic, like a child scanning a busy strip-mall for a lost guardian.

On a small incline of grass about twenty feet from her, an old man sat in a beam of sunlight that filtered in from between two trees.

He was portly with a slightly receding hairline of gray hair coming to a small crown of smooth skin at the peak of his scalp. He was wearing a purple button-down shirt that was rolled up at the cuffs, and khaki shorts. He was smiling at her, in that expectant way that people did when they wanted to start a conversation with a stranger.

For a moment Crowley flirted with the idea of smiling in return, but never quite made it to the act, the fluttering discomfort growing from its consistent home between her breasts until it overcame her, tingling its way across her flesh with petals that were delicate, yet sharp.

She got up suddenly, and made her way back into the building.

As soon as she rose, the pigeon took flight as well, disappearing suddenly into the bright light of day.

Marjorie Simmons sat behind the large, tall desk that took up the majority of the same in the LA Sun's lobby. While sitting she was dwarfed by it, only the stray tufts of her platinum blonde hair visible until one stepped right up to the glass and looked down at her.

The desk wasn't made for the type on security that had been grafted onto it like a prosthetic limb. It was the type of large mahogany mammoth things that was put in during the construction of a building and never moved:

carved from a single piece of wood and worked to a fine finish. It looked as though it were a part of the floor, with no visible feet or gaps between the two. It had been retro-fitted with bulletproof clear Plexiglas windows that stretched from floor to ceiling all the way around it, terminating behind Marjorie in a large metal door. In front of her, flush with the uppermost edge of the desk, was a long rectangle for passing forms back and forth. Just above it a speaker protruded from the glass, attached to a large microphone that sat on Marjorie's desk via a series of clumsy and winding cables.

Xander had been standing at the gap in the glass for a full two minutes before she looked up and acknowledged him. Her eyes were small slices in her head, almost concealing the bloodshot whites of them. Her fingers didn't jolt when she moved from one keyboard to another, and there was no stale savory smell of marijuana on her breath that Xander could detect, so he assumed that the soreness of her eyes were a by-product of a long night of great stress.

He didn't allow himself to feel remorse that he was about to add to it.

Lisa stood just behind him and to his left. If Marjorie hadn't noticed that they'd come in together, she would have been forgiven for thinking that Lisa was another patient in line, whose arrival was separate from Xander's.

Marjorie met Xander's eye... at least he thought she did; they were closed so tight it was hard to tell. Her skin was pale and placid, winding tributaries of blue veins moving throughout her cheeks. They seemed to swell and recess with every breath she took, although the cheeks seemed to remain stationary, in some bizarre optical illusion that Xander could not – and did not wish to – understand.

After what felt like an eternity of awkward silence, Xander spoke. "I'm here about Luka Patel?"

Her head lowered and she brought the thumb and forefinger of her left hand up to massage the bridge of her nose, then lowered it again. She moved slightly to the left, allowing her hands to rest in the ready position above the keyboard of the laptop that, based on the dust that had settled behind it, was a permanent fixture of the desk. "Name?" she said, her voice shrill and nasal.

"Luka..." Xander said, raising an eyebrow. "Luka Patel." Beneath what was visible from behind the desk, Xander placed his hand in his jeans pocket. He withdrew it a moment later, his fingers clasped tight.

"*Your* name?" Marjorie repeated, with emphasis, making no effort to disguise her aversion to doing so.

"Ah, Michael Kennessy with Homicide 12," Xander said. He extended his hand through the glass. Marjorie looked at it, then back to the laptop, and typed several keys in quick succession.

Lisa looked from Xander to Marjorie quizzically, but did not speak.

"I don't see you in here, Mr. Kennessy."

"*Detective* Kennessy," Xander corrected, withdrawing his hand. He'd stuck it through to the point where it threatened to become wedged at his bicep, making it three-quarters of the way to Marjorie's head, but no farther. She hadn't flinched, as if knowing he wouldn't have been able to reach her even if that had been his intent.

"Is this going to take long?" Lisa asked in an annoyed

tone she'd practised before they'd come in.

Marjorie ignored her. "There's no Detective Kennessy in here either. We spoke to the police today; Detective Hynes was in."

"From Missing Persons, yes. He's from Twelve as well," he said with a confidence he did not have, and behind him Lisa struggled to maintain her appearance of impatience. "They asked me to come down and have a look as well, see if there's anything that jumps out at me." His eyes went from Marjorie to the laptop, and then back again. It was a new model, the type of slimmed-down design with only a few solitary jacks along one side. The other computer was hidden within the desk somewhere with only its screen and keyboard and their accompanying gaggle of wires visible.

"Is there a reason Homicide is looking into this?" Marjorie asked, raising her eyebrow enough that Xander finally caught the glimpse of a violet pupil.

"Is there a reason you think we shouldn't be?" Xander pantomimed reaching into his pocket for a pad and pen that he did not have. "Marjorie, right?"

She frowned and went back to her laptop. "There's nothing here."

"I have an appointment I need to get to," Lisa spoke up, craning her neck so that she could see Marjorie over Xander's shoulder. "Is this going to take long? Sir, do you mind if I go --"

"You're going to have to step back, Miss," Xander said, taking both hands out of his pockets and turning slightly toward Lisa. "Police business."

"Yeah, don't 'Miss' me," Lisa scoffed, and Xander

wasn't certain if it was a part of her act or not.

He rolled his eyes and turned back away from Lisa, leaning in closer to Marjorie. "Is there someone else I can speak to to move this along?"

"I don't have an appointment and nobody else is --"

"Don't you turn away from me!"

"It's surely not just you here."

"The only other people are on watch and can't come off until --"

"I pay your salary!"

"Just one moment," Marjorie said, pushing back from her desk as though the extra arms-length away from the mounting chaos on the opposite side of the glass separated her from it. She got up awkwardly in the claustrophobic space the sides of the desk allowed. "I'll see if there's anyone who can verify your appointment."

"Oh, that's great," Lisa said, flopping her hands to her sides dramatically. "This is going to take forever now."

"Ma'am, I assure you it'll just be a --"

"Don't *you* 'Ma'am' me, either!" Lisa huffed, her voice growing hoarse.

"Simmer down," Xander said, beneath his breath but so that everyone involved could hear.

Marjorie grasped at the card key that hung from her belt and pulled at it. It was attached to her with a zip-tie that made a sharp whirring sound as she brought it to the sensor alongside the door. The red LED alongside it turned green, and an instant later she was gone and the door had slammed shut behind her.

Xander turned to face Lisa immediately, holding up the thumb drive he'd had palmed in his hand since removing it from his pocket. "Good work, I need you to get this into the laptop." He pressed a trigger on the drive and the metal connector snapped out of its protective base.

Lisa lowered her eyes at him, her lips pursed. "You don't 'Miss' me," she said curtly, taking the thumb drive and stepping past him.

"Not as long as you stick around, I won't," he said under his breath. She ignored him, awkwardly bending down so that her shoulder was parallel with the gap in the glass, to get the most reach out of it. Beside her, Xander stood atop his toes to look down over the edge of the desk, trying to see what she was doing from a vantage point she couldn't. "A little left. Make sure it's tongue-end up."

Lisa let out a huff, the strain of the awkward stance making sweat dot her brow already. "How'd you know she'd leave?"

"What was she going to do, call security? On a cop?" He paused. "Left. Seriously, more left. All the left."

She bobbed her head in acknowledgement, sticking her tongue out of the side of her mouth.

"Would you want to get in the middle of a spat between an LA cop and an obviously pregnant woman? Most people have a fervent need not to end up on the evening news."

She turned to him, so fast her hair bobbed. "I'm sorry: *obviously* pregnant?"

"You've got it," he said, ignoring her retort. "Put it in."

She pushed in the thumb drive. The screen on the laptop popped back to life after having fallen into its sleep mode, the speech-bubble announcing that it had found the drive announcing itself in the lower right-hand corner of the screen.

Xander's gaze moved to the LED light alongside the security door, still the same red it had been ever since Marjorie closed it behind her.

Lisa started to withdraw her hand.

"No no," Xander said quickly, raising both hands. "Don't leave."

She turned to him with her mouth agape. "I can't just stay here like this! What if she comes back?"

"I'm keeping an eye."

"This isn't an easy position to stay in."

He stepped up behind her to help take some of the weight off her legs.

"That wasn't an invitation!"

He backed off again, returning to his vantage point above the laptop's monitor.

The LED light to the right of the door turned green.

"Take it out!" he hissed through gritted teeth. "Take it out!"

Lisa grabbed the thumb drive and pulled, the laptop moving a full inch toward her before it let go, making a trail in the dust on the desk. When it came loose, she slipped backward and Xander jolted forward, catching her by the armpit before she could fall against her backside. He pulled her back to her feet briskly, spinning around as he did and coming to a stop back at the desk just as Marjorie appeared in the doorway.

She eyed Xander, then Lisa, whose cheeks were red and flushed with sweat.

"No one has any word of any appointment to see you,

Detective," Marjorie said in an agitated tone. "But if you'd like to leave your name and --"

"Waste of my time," Xander frowned, rapping one knuckle against the desk before turning to leave.

Marjorie lowered her eyes at him as she watched him leave, then turned to Lisa and forced herself to smile politely. "Sorry about the wait; what can I do for you?"

Lisa stared at her for a long moment. After several blank-faced breaths, she asked if she could use the bathroom.

The cafe that looked across at the LA Sun was named The Quicksand. It had been there for two years, and when they had first gotten the space it had been a sleek white technology provider with no right angles in its corners. The owners of The Quicksand had quickly plastered over all that. They bought malformed bricks from a local construction site, leaving large chunks undone. They plastered, but purposefully made some variations of the mixture too thick and others too thin to achieve that perfectly imperfect, uneven aesthetic of amateur that their target market sorely craved.

Each table was a high-seater, designed so that only the tallest of the tall could comfortably sit at it and touch the ground. Built into the top of each was a screen that rose from the table, the surface of the table itself a touch-sensitive glass screen, the keys pressed between panes in vinyl. Xander had priced one of those keyboards once, and at the time it would have run well over two hundred dollars. If he tried, he could feel the seams where it met the glass tabletop, but only with great effort.

He sat at a table against the far back wall, in a darkened corner where the bricks had been arranged in an inconvenient way that blocked the light. His table was along a through-line that the baristas used to get into the back to fetch soups or cold sandwiches, but he found as long as he kept his eyes on the screen they treated him as though he was invisible. That was an important part of the social contract in the Screen-Age: eyes on screens meant 'shields up.' Do not disturb. Annoy at own risk.

His fingers hovered over the keyboard and trackpad, not typing much but occasionally pecking out the occasional snap with his fingers, commands that he'd long since adopted as second-nature changing the layout on the screen minutely. There were four video feeds on the screen, each taking up roughly a quadrant of it; although he had manoeuvred the screen in the upper right to take up just a little more room than the rest. The people on them moved in the jerky, forced motion that came from missing frames played on increased speed, each person going about their day. In the top left, a woman was making beds: many beds, all in a row, repeating the same practiced motions to make each one.

"That was incredibly awkward," Lisa said, pulling out the chair next to Xander. Her hair was in front of her eyes from the walk over – although only across the street, she had to go a half-click up the street in order to reach the crosswalk, then return. "There had to have been a better way to do that."

"Probably," Xander admitted, his hands clasped in front of his mouth and his eyes not leaving the screen.

Her head twitched. She watched him as he watched

the screen, tiny flecks of crimson filling his cheeks more and more. His pupils slid back and forth in his head as they moved from one window to the next. She pulled her chair around from across from him to alongside him, and finally sat down. "What are we watching?"

The woman making the beds had moved on to vacuuming, pushing a large machine with a gargantuan trap between the cots. The space between the beds was so scant that the vacuum shifted the beds to either side of it slightly when she pushed it through, only to be shifted back when she came to the next gap, and so on.

"Xander?"

"Right now, I'm watching a bunch of people who would make my shit-list if I didn't have like, five more important things on my plate at all times." He pointed from the woman on feed one vacuuming to the man on feed two arranging a learning activity in the yard, then to one of an old woman cooking lunch, and finally to the receptionist they'd just met. "It's been ten hours since the kid went missing, at this point. Five since they've been up and active, and there's still no sign they've noticed he's gone."

Lisa frowned. "Horrible," she said. She leaned toward Xander to stop some of the glare from the counter. He flinched, but said nothing. "You know when he was taken then?"

He held down the glass above the control and alt keys and tapped M with a resigned sigh, his mouth warbling as though at war with itself. All four feeds changed, though their angles and basic composure remained the same. Children appeared in the beds of frame one as though reality had opened up and spat them there, and the light dimmed in the other three feeds. The time codes had jumped to ten hours earlier, almost to the minute.

In Feed One, at the third bed from the top, fourteen-year-old Luka Patel was sitting up in his bed bolt upright, unable to sleep.

"That's the one," Xander said brusquely, motioning with a nod of his head. He pressed play at the bottom of the window. "Watch."

The footage was static for a what felt like an eternity, so much so that were it not for the timer counting its way along, Lisa would have sworn she was looking at a still image. The picture shuddered and shook, its bluish hue interrupted by the crashing greens and red of artifacting files as it played – the modern equivalent of the vertical-hold lines that made old videotape such unnerving to watch.

Lisa leaned in and squinted, watching as Luka's small chest moved up and down in regular intervals, his shoulders hunching and falling as he did. "What am I --" looking for, Lisa was going to ask, before the sharp line of rectangular light sliced its way through the right side of the screen. It was a rip in reality, a tear so bright and sudden that the lens of the camera flared for a moment, as if it was stunned by the sudden intrusion of light. "Fuck!" she snapped, leaning back from the monitor, startled. She pushed Xander's shoulder. "You could have warned me."

Xander glared at the screen. "Keep watching."

As the camera's aperture readjusted itself to the new light source, a figure in the light began to emerge. There was a man, a slender man standing in the doorway, his shadow cast just as long as the light from the door he'd opened. He appeared as if from nowhere, the shadow not stepping into the doorframe but fading from it, as though particles of darkness were flooding into place.

Luka had moved. He had turned to face whomever cast the shadow.

They were stuck again in that position, still except for the small movements of Luka's chest. The lens flare had hidden the frame of motion, bringing Luka immediately from one position to the next, like animation missing its in-betweens.

Lisa felt the wispy hair along her arm stand on end.

The shadow moved. Only its head at first, then the arms in subtle, stiff motions, a marionette in a silent film. As they watched, Luka began to speak silently, his mouth moving in jarring frames.

Lisa squinted, leaning back in. "No sound?"

"He's asking if his mother was released."

When she turned back to him, her eyes were wet. She swallowed. "You can read lips?"

He didn't respond. He stared at the screen as Luka got up from his bed and walked off the screen in the direction of the light, his shadow merging with the other until the door was closed and darkness penetrated the room again. "Now there," he said, motioning to the other feed. It showed a long hallway that branched off into another. Across that gap, as if on cue, two shadows passed. Xander pointed to the third feed, the one that led out to the main corridor they'd been in. There was a worker at the desk and after several arduous moments, they got up and left.

As soon as one door closed, a second opened, and Luka stepped through.

The other figure stepped through as well now, visible for the first time. It was a male and tall, but by no means as tall as the shadow had implied. His limbs were lanky and his clothes ill-fitting. He was in the frame for only a moment, and then both were gone. The timestamp was 03:52.

"So that's it then?" Lisa asked, standing erect. "We don't know what happened to them after leaving the home?"

Xander gave her a wry look. "Please," he said, as he closed down the camera feeds one by one. When he was at the desktop (a scenic sunset of purples and pinks, branded with The Quicksand logo), he pressed the wireless button in the lower right-hand corner of the screen. A thin window popped up, cutting through the pink the same way the light from the door had sliced through the dark. It was a list of networks, each one with the wireless symbol on it showing a different number of bars, each with a tiny lock next to it. He pointed to the list. "The computers here run on wireless. We're connected to one for the cafe, but we don't have to be. We can connect to anything within range."

There was a long list of wireless access points.

Quicksand Wifi

SportsShop Wifi

WholeFoods Wifi

LAVapor Wifi

WC-D52X

KoreaNail Wifi

WC-5000 DX

CC-PF 20

CC-DX1

MDCC-5001

Lisa looked over the list, then looked over it again. "I don't get it. Ours is strongest, and we don't know the passwords to the others."

Xander smiled. "Watch the news much?"

"As little as possible, why?"

He clicked WC-D52X, which had the strongest signal of those without coded names. It called up a box asking for the username and password. He highlighted the network name, opened a web browser, and pasted it in. "There was this story a while back about foreign internet porn companies posting up video of American girls in locker rooms and such. Voyeur stuff, the modern day equivalent of the guys who drill holes in change-room walls."

"That's sick," Lisa said with a curled lip. Her hand went to her abdomen.

Xander bobbed his head. "It is what it is." He clicked the third link down on the search results that came up, quickly scrolled through the data and specs on the screen, then highlighted a long string of letters and numbers. "The point is, how did they do that? How did they get their hands on footage from our kids from half a world away?" He clicked on the WC-D52X wireless access point. It popped up asking for a password, and he pasted in the long string of letters and numbers. The password prompt box went away and the hourglass icon began to spin. "They could do it because most companies buy their camera systems off store shelves, and way too many don't change the default username and passwords." The hourglass went away and a window opened on the screen that was a video of a cafe with malformed bricks and high tables and chairs.

Lisa stiffened.

"Say hello." Xander waved. An instant later on the video, a man sitting next to a woman at a chair in the back corner of the cafe waved.

Lisa looked up into the far corner, spotting the tiny lens she'd missed. She turned back to the feed quickly enough to make eye contact with herself, standing in the back of the room. The result was unnerving and sent a fresh chill down her spine. "So every one of those is a camera?" She motioned to the list of wireless networks.

"A camera system. It might just be one camera, it might be one parent camera and a few children." He disconnected himself from the WC-D52X network and back to the Quicksand Wifi, then called up the web browser again. "Attaching to the camera's wireless only gets you that one parent camera feed, and you have to be near enough to the camera to do it, so that's not a huge security risk." He typed in a web address and hit enter. It came up to a wireless camera system. In the username he typed in WC-D52X, then switched to the previous window and copied the long password again. "To get the rest and to get the backlog of record, you have to log into the online system. You can do that from anywhere in the world, so if you're the boss you can keep an eye on the employees from home, or Aruba, or... wherever."

"And nobody changes the default password," Lisa said.

Xander smiled at her and pressed enter. Seven icons came up, the main one showing the angle of the cafe that they'd seen by connecting to the camera's wifi network. Another showed a different angle of the cafe, and another one was a straight-on view of the cash counter, while another one was a top-down angle looking down at the cash register. One was pointed from a vantage-point just above the cash counter out to the bay window at the front of the cafe, looking out at the LA Sun.

He clicked on it. It came up to the current feed of that camera, showing the people at the register at this very moment, and the window beyond that, and the front doors to the LA Sun beyond that. There was a text-box in the lower left-hand corner with a time-stamp in it that counted the current date and time with a pause button next to it. He clicked in the box and typed in 03:52 for the time and hit play.

The people in the feed disappeared and the tone changed, the natural light of the window snapping off as though he'd flicked a switch.

Lisa leaned in. "This is... wow."

The clock ticked by, and after a moment two figures came out of the LA Sun building. They paused briefly, then turned right and exited the frame at a jogger's gate.

"They went east," Xander said matter-of-factly. He called up a new window and opened a city map that immediately stuck a red pin in their current location. He zoomed in until he could see the text overlaying the blocks that represented the buildings they were in clearly. The next business to the east of the Sun was LA Vapor.

He minimized the map and opened the wireless access

point list again. LA Vapor's wireless had 3.5 bars at medium strength, and so did the CC-DX1 camera wireless. He opened a new browser window and repeated the same steps as he had before, looking up the default name and password of the camera system. Sure enough, a new selection of angles and timestamps appeared on the screen. One camera framed the storefront window perfectly and Xander entered it, again changing the timestamp to 3:52.

After a moment's hesitation, the shadowy male stepped into frame. He was almost out of it again when he stopped and turned around, realizing Luka wasn't behind him.

"Come on, kid, turn and run," Xander said under his breath, and Lisa wasn't entirely certain he'd intended to say it out loud.

Luka stepped into view, his hands muddled together in a mass of pixels near his solar plexus. When he stopped both males were on either edge of the screen, the backwards R of the word 'Vapor' obscuring the unknown face, but it was easy to tell from the body language that he was speaking.

Luka took a step forward, then back two, almost out of frame in the direction of the LA Sun building again.

The unknown male reached out his hand palm up, and after a moment's hesitation, Luka stepped forward and took it and they both disappeared off screen.

"Fuck," Xander said, and was about to close the window again.

"Wait," Lisa interrupted, jolting a hand forward. "Go back... can you make it go back?"

Xander eyed her, then clicked a button with two triangles on it. The video started to play in reverse, frame by frame. Slowly, Luka and the other person backed up into view.

"Stop," Lisa said, touching his shoulder.

Both Luka and the other person were about the exit the frame in the still, their arms cocked at awkward angles as though they were about to break into a run. Their hands were clasped between them and in the grainy footage they were both shadowed. If they hadn't watch the footage from the start, it might have been difficult to tell them apart.

"Do you see it?" Lisa asked.

Xander looked at her, then back at the screen, his brow furrowed. "No."

She reached out and touched the screen, pressing on Luka's head and then dragging her finger over to the stranger's and back again. "They're the same height."

Xander squinted, looking from one to the other.

"The person who came and got him was a child."

They watched on different feeds as the boys went past the Whole Foods and the Samwise Sport Shop on the corner. They'd turned on the corner and gone down the alley behind the shop and it had taken Xander a few moments to find an angle that showed it. They'd stopped by a garbage bin so that the strange boy could have a cigarette, the light outside the back door giving the first clear look at him. He was blond and gaunt with dark rings under his eyes and the type of sunken, bony cheeks that Xander hadn't had for many years.

Luka had turned away again while the other boy was finishing his smoke, but the boy caught him and said something.

"It's not far now," Xander said, in time with the boy's lips.

When they exited the frame, Xander found an angle for the back entrance of the Korean Nail and Massage Parlor. The frame stayed stagnant for several moments until Luka and the strange boy entered the frame.

They stood there and waited. They waited so long that Xander turned on the fast forward option, clicking it three times to speed up its rate until eventually the boys both disappeared.

"Stop!" Lisa exclaimed.

He dialed back the timestamp slowly, until both boys were back where they had been waiting, and pressed play.

From the shadows to the right of the frame, a tall woman stepped into view. She towered over the other two, cementing in Lisa's theory that they were both children: it was not that Luka was tall for his age, but that both boys were teens.

The woman was a platinum blonde and let her hair fall down around her shoulders. Her dress was the deep shade of red that women in noir mysteries always wore. There was a slash of the same red across her lips, blurred and distorted by the pixilation of the image.

"Who's that?" Lisa asked, turning from the screen to Xander.

The blonde woman brought her hand up into Luka's hair and ran them through it as though she'd known him her whole life... as though she owned him. Her nails stuck out against the dark of his hair, the same bright crimson of her dress. Her lips parted in a smile and she took Luka by the arm with great force. He finally tried to pull away, but her grip on him was tight.

The other boy lit another cigarette as Luka was dragged out of the frame, and walked off after them.

"Xander?" Lisa said, staring at the newly blank image again.

He clicked back several frames until the woman was centered in it again, and paused. Her smile was large and her eyes so wide their lids had disappeared completely. He'd caught her just at the moment when she had grabbed Luka's arm and wretched it to one side, her face a terrifying mix of anger and glee all at once.

"That's definitely not Fields," he said under his breath.

CHAPTER SIX

The elevator doors opened with an audible ping, revealing the vast-yet-cramped department that was Homicide 12. Duncan stepped in and took a deep breath before continuing past the hall into the bullpen proper.

The Homicide division of any city was busy, but the twelve located in Los Angeles offered a completely new level of confusion. The room was a living, breathing entity under the always-hot sun, moving and pulsing with excitement, energy, and need. The walls seemed to expand and contract with the heat, as though they were breathing.

There were three offices separate from the main floor. The rest of the floor was a one massive and open office with glass walls on all sides, making the halls around it and the Los Angeles sky constantly visible. Thirty-something desks were arranged around the room like Jenga blocks, all of them the same but for a few that were stained different colours. Most had long scrapes running across their finish from multiple moves, and all were covered in case files, family photos, or both.

Duncan stood in the vacant space that stretched out from the entrance, surveying the desks around him. Most were in use by people too busy to even notice he was there. Some had phones pressed to their ears, others were going over files, and most were typing at computers. More than one person was doing all three.

He worked his gum around his mouth and took all this in, his gaze finally settling on a closed office door on the other side of the room.

"Fed?" came a high voice to his lower left.

He turned and found that his hip was less than a foot from the corner of someone's desk, the owner of which appeared to be a brunette woman with a phone pressed hard enough to her ear to leave an indentation mark like a streak of crimson all the way down her face. She had a pen in one hand and was balancing a pad of paper against her calf; her chair leaned back against the thick window behind her. She was looking up at him.

"Excuse me?" he asked, stepping closer to the desk.

"Are – you – the – Fed?" she said, each word annunciated clearly and with a faint taste of condescension.

He nodded, wiped his palm on his shirt, then extended it to her. "Yea. Duncan Taggart, I'm --"

"Desk," she cut him off, motioning behind him with the top of her pen before using it to scribble something else down. "I'm still here."

He frowned and rescinded his hand, then turned in the direction she'd motioned.

There was a desk there that was empty, with nothing on it but a clean shiny new finish. There were no placemats that doubled as calendars, no Rolodex, and no brightly coloured folders. The only things on the desk were a computer and a single file folder. When he stepped over to it, he noticed that there was a rectangular splotch near the front of the desk that was darker than the rest. Something had rested on it for so long that it had shielded it from the rays of light streaming in through the windows, and when everything else had become sun-bleached, it had stayed as dark as a tumor.

He walked over to it and placed his hand on its surface, feeling the cold contours of the wood grain beneath his calloused, rough fingertips, then sat down at it with a sigh.

He caught the woman who had pointed out the desk watching him as he adjusted the chair. She looked away when they made eye contact and said something else to whomever she was talking to, something completely inaudible among the roar of Homicide 12.

To his right was a large bald man whose badge looked to be clinging to his belt for dear life. The beige pants he wore seemed to be splitting at the seams, the threads being pulled apart like the childhood of an alcoholic adolescent.

He turned back to the file that had been laid perfectly in the center of his desk, and opened it.

It was a folder on Rae Stevens, a banker who had been killed several weeks ago, according to the file. He'd been stabbed in a busy city street less than a mile from where he'd worked and left in the mouth of an alley, and still it had taken the passer-bys hours to notice that something was amiss.

There was an autopsy report attached from the same

twerk-eyed pathologist that had helped him earlier, and it seemed as though all three had been killed with similar weapons. Hair and fibres had been sent to trace, but in Duncan's experience very few cases in real life were solved by hair and fibre. Cases were solved by finding connections, knowing human behavior, and suppressing the all-too-human urge to not ask uncomfortable questions.

He went through the file as much as his stomach could handle, then closed it again.

He spent several minutes adjusting his chair, which was one of those bargain-basement adjustable ones that never adjusted in ways that were user-friendly. He pressed the lever he thought would make his rise and jolted down half a foot, so he pressed it the other way only to fall another foot, and eventually gave up and stood back from it. He gave its rightmost wheel a tap with his foot out of spite, and the chair lolled away from him slowly before coming to a rest, leaning against the desk and mocking him.

He turned to the obese man to his right, who was presently typing a handwritten witness testimony into the computer using the 'hunt and peck' method of keyboard use.

"What's the deal with the chairs?" Duncan asked, striding up until his midsection rested on the lip of the man's chair. The marker on his desk read Detective Jeff Mason. "Some kind of lowest-bidder scam I'm missing out of or what?"

Mason took a second to notice Duncan, doing a double take: the first glance to see where the distraction was coming from, and the second to confirm, yes, he was standing right next to me. "Pardon?"

"The chairs," Duncan said again, motioning over his back with his thumb. "Why are the chairs here so horrible?" He paused, smirked, then extended his hand. "Duncan Taggart."

Mason took it, briefly, then turned back to his work. "Mason," he said under his breath, almost as an afterthought.

"Right, so Mason, I'm working this --"

"Just a second," Mason said, raising a finger. He then aimed that finger back at the keys and continued to type.

Duncan waited several seconds before realizing that 'a second' meant 'until I'm done, and maybe not even then.' He frowned, walked back to his desk, eyed the folder, then turned and walked back to the woman across the gap from him, who had hung up her phone and now had her notepad propped up between her keyboard and screen. Her hands hovered over the keyboard with her thumbs balanced over each alt key, ready to type when the need arose, her wrists balanced on a cushion that ran along the bottom edge of her desk.

He leaned back to look at her marker, pressed along the front of her desk in vinyl. She was Detective Janet Nesbit.

"That's a mouthful," he smirked, thrusting his hands into his pockets.

She focused her large brown eyes on him, evaluating him as though she hadn't spoken to him a few minutes before. She didn't move her head when she regarded him, just her eyes, and had moved them back to her screen before she spoke. "Pardon?"

"Nesbit. Sounds like you make cookies in a tree or something."

She tilted her head to one side as she typed something in, but did not look at him. "Who's to say I don't?" She smirked a little.

He leaned forward. "Can you tell me the deal with the medical examiner? The one with the eye. What kind of work does he do?"

That got her to look. "Autopsies, mostly."

"Yeah, I get that. I mean is he good at them, because I'm working this case – I got assigned this Shane case –"

"I know what case you were assigned."

"Okay, and there's nothing on the bodies yet that really tells me what happened, and I'm one of those guys who usually goes for the body first. So I'm --"

"In the middle of something," Janet said, pointing to the screen.

Duncan stopped.

"Right now. I am in the middle of something. It's not Fed work, but it's just as important, I'm sure."

He straightened. "I didn't mean to imply that--"

"Seriously, right in the middle," she interjected again, tapping several keys as if to pantomime work.

Duncan stepped back a pace from her desk. He turned back toward the file, just in view, staring up at him from his assigned seat with the horrid chair, then back to Nesbit's desk, then turned to the door he'd come in through to his left.

He took his hand out of his pocket, withdrawing his cigarette, and placed it behind his ear. "Yeah, fuck this," he said under his breath, and left Homicide 12 the way he'd come in.

Janet watched him for a moment until the elevator doors closed, then went back to her search.

The office of M.Ed Susan Bright was massive and bare. There was a small desk crammed into one wall with a flat screen TV mounted just above it, and a small filing cabinet with two drawers next to that. Between that and the far wall twenty feet away, there were only two uncomfortable chairs and a small desk with three legs that wobbled, and may have been meant to have four originally.

The room was mainly used for group therapy, Susan had explained, as she'd set up the chairs across from one another. She made coffee from a pod percolator in the hall and offered Crowley one. Crowley had accepted, then amended to decaf.

Crowley had been sipping the decaf – with far too much cream added – for almost four minutes, with nothing but the sound of the ticking clock on the wall to their right and the slow, uneven hum of the computer's fan.

"Sometimes it helps to try and explain why you're here?" Susan said. She was holding a pen that was resting on a yellow legal pad, which was in turn propped against a metal clipboard. It looked serious, somehow – moreso than a wooden clipboard would have.

Crowley warbled her mouth, tried to answer twice, then stopped.

"By which I mean, what you hope to accomplish from therapy."

Crowley nodded. "Well, there's, this boy."

Susan wrote something down.

"No, not like that. Really."

Susan looked at her and smiled, but didn't say anything or amend what she had written.

"Okay, let's... let's back up. That was a dumb thing to say." She was fidgeting with her hands, sorting them as if sorting her thoughts.

"Are you here because you want to be here?"

Crowley raised an eyebrow, then looked to one side as if she'd see a camera there. "Well... I'm here. Nobody dragged me in here."

She smiled. "Some people are here for themselves, and those people tend to get a lot out of therapy. Some are court mandated or doctor recommended to be here, and we do what we can, but that's an uphill battle... and then some people are here because their spouse or partner is pressuring them to be here. One too many fights that ended with being told they needed 'mental help,'" she made air quotes with her fingers "for their opinions or stances or argument style."

Crowley's brow furrowed, and she worked her tongue around her mouth and looked away.

Susan made a brief note, which couldn't have been more than a single character. "Is there anything like that happening?"

"No," Crowley said flatly.

Susan watched her for a moment, until Crowley met her eye, and even then a moment longer. "Let's come back to that, then? Who should we contact in case of emergency?"

"Lisa Rowdan."

"Number?"

She gave it.

"Relationship?"

"Roommate."

"Any recent medical issues or hospitalizations?"

"No."

"Are you on any medications currently?"

"No."

"And what about recreational drugs?"

"Not for years, and never seriously."

Susan nodded. "Are you religious?"

Crowley winced. It got her attention, breaking her out of the drone of her answers. "What?"

"Some people want it worked into their therapy."

"Oh," Crowley straightened, then shrugged. "No."

Susan smiled. "Me neither," she winked.

Crowley's shoulders reloosened, looser than they had been before the misstep.

"Any familial history of mental illness?"

Crowley tightened again, but did not answer.

Susan waited.

"I think so. I'm not sure. None diagnosed."

Susan nodded, and made a notation. When she was done, she put down the pen and smiled, crossing her arms and leaning forward onto her knee. "What's your end goal to get out of this?"

She was silent again for a long moment. There were tissues on the table between them alongside their coffees. She didn't need one, but wanted to need them. It felt like the right answer to that question was behind a plug, and that the plug was made of tears, and that if she could just cry and babble all her feelings as they came she could get it out... but she had no desire to cry. No *emotional* desire, only a cognitive one.

Susan pushed the box closer to Crowley with the tip of her finger, noticing where she was looking.

"There's this boy..." Crowley started again. Her lip twitched and was almost a smirk, but was gone quickly. "A guy. Is there an age limit on calling a male a boy?"

"I think most men would say so."

Crowley smirked. She was funny. The smile only lasted a moment, and then was gone again. "I want to be able to make *choices*," she said finally. It came out all at once, like word vomit, her hand circling in front of her to pantomime the words coming out of her. Someone watching the interaction on mute might have thought she'd been indicating 'large breasts.' "Everyone around me makes choices and I feel like I just... can't. About anything. Sometimes I can fake it, but most of the time I'm just... following along." She paused. Her throat was parched, so she took some of her coffee... and then all of it. She hadn't meant to, but after a moment the tiny cup was dry. She didn't put it down, instead cradling it in her lap, her thumbs pressing neatly around its edges. "We've been arguing... not really, that's not the right word. Playfully ribbing? Flirtatiously antagonizing? I don't know. I'm not sure how he feels about it, but there's no sense asking him because I can't make the *choice* of how I feel about it."

"Are feelings a choice?"

Crowley's eyes narrowed. "They can be, I think, yeah. I think you can choose to overlook someone's bad qualities, or choose to stay away from someone with too many bad ones."

Susan nodded and smiled. It was a big smile. "I think that's true, but rarely do people do it."

"I guess that's what I mean when I say it's about a boy, but... not, all at once. It's not that I want him... it's that I want to figure out *if* I want him... am I saying that right?"

"You're saying it fine."

"But not even figure just that out. That'd be a pretty shallow reason to come to therapy."

"I've heard worse."

Crowley smirked with her tongue in her cheek. "No, I... want to be able to choose, in general. I want to be that person who makes choices instead becomes paralyzed. I want that... what's the word?"

"Agency?"

"*Yes*," Crowley said, snapping her fingers and pointing at her. "That's it exactly. Such a college way of saying it, but yes. That works. Agency."

Susan wrote down 'Agency' and circled it.

"It's not about him. It has nothing to do with him, it's a me thing. I just... I want to decide whether or not to make a move before he does. Because if he makes the move first and I go along, then I'm just... going along. I didn't make the choice then, and I don't know where I am then. Where I'll be."

Susan nodded. "No, that makes sense. So would it be fair to say that you'd like to be more decisive?"

She paused. "I guess."

Susan paused, then put the pen down into the gap cut

for it in the metal clipboard and put both down on the table between them. "What other types of choices do you have a hard time making?"

Crowley winced. "I was at the grocery store a few weeks ago with Lisa, and she asked me to go get cereal. That's simple, right? Only she didn't tell me what kind of cereal, she just said: cereal. So I go over to the cereal aisle... have you been in the cereal aisle lately?"

"I have a three year old."

"Oh, then you know. There's way too many brands! Too many brands. There's just this avalanche of them: Lucky Charms and Special K and Froot Loops and Harvest Crunch... and every different type has an off-brand that the store makes to be like, a knock-off of the main brand, and I swear now there are knock-offs of the knock-offs, each one for like a dollar cheaper than the other." She swallowed. Without realizing it, she'd started to tear up. "So I'm there in this sea of colours and they all start to just... blend together. All of them are just in this swirl." She swirled her fingers around either temple, then without elaborating as to a different feeling, pressed them into side of her head. "Lisa came and got me a few minutes later and she just picked Cheerios... she just picked it, like it was nothing. She doesn't even *like* Cheerios, really, she just: made the choice and lived with cereal she didn't one hundred percent like for a few days. I *wish* I could do that."

Susan picked up her pen and wrote something. She looked at it for a moment, then turned to Crowley and made a smile that Crowley instinctively knew was less than genuine. "When was the last time you remember making a choice?"

Crowley winced. "I don't know. Define choice, I guess."

"When did you first notice this being an issue?"

She turned, each hand retreating to the opposite bicep. Susan did not fill the silence, she let it drag, until eventually Crowley looked up and smirked. "There's this story I love growing up... apparently it's a classic, but I read it for years as a children's book called 'The Knight and the Bride.' It wasn't until I got older that I learned it wasn't just some fable, it was from *The Canterbury Tales*."

"The Wife of Bath's Tale?"

Crowley nodded. "It's about this knight who marries this woman who's been cursed. She has to spend half the day ugly and the other half beautiful. So on their wedding night, she gives the knight the choice: he can choose which half of the day she spend as each. Does he want her to be pretty in bed for him and then ugly out in public when they're out with society? Or does he want someone who's beautiful out in public so that others envy him and only ugly at night, when it's just them? So the Knight says he doesn't care, that the choice is hers... and that breaks the spell, because he gives her what all women want: the power of choice." She met Susan's gaze. "I want the ability to choose."

Susan smiled, wrote something, then leaned forward. "We can get you in more than once a week, if you'd like?"

Crowley nodded.

CHAPTER SEVEN

Xander jammed the map into the upper corner of the wall. It curled back twice and each time he shoved it back with increasing force, the final time shoving a blue thumb tack in to hold it. He smoothed creases and pinned the rough paper at every joint. It crumpled and bunched and tried to refold itself in places, the peaks and valleys of the page making it a wildly inaccurate topographical map.

He stepped back when he pushed in his last thumb tack. It had taken an entire ten pack, and even still, the map was fighting them to succumb to gravity. It was a large map of the greater Los Angeles area, and it now took up the entire western wall of his living room.

The heel of his foot landed on a stack of paper thirty leafs high, but he ignored it. He continued back until he could see the entirety of the map, his back almost all the way back to his bedroom door. He reached into his pocket and pulled out a small canister of pins with different coloured tops: red, yellow, and green. He shook three out into his opposite palm, knelt down, and picked up a sheet of paper.

The page had a greyscale photo of a young boy on it, and a caption: Dylan Porter, age ten.

The details given alongside the missing person's bulletin were sparse. He'd been last seen wearing a blue and white striped shirt and denim pants. He was blond and had blue eyes, and in the photo he was missing one of his eye teeth. He'd been last seen on a security camera at the Diamond Springs strip-mall outside a Tire and Oil-Change Drop-Off thirteen days after he'd initially disappeared. He'd been staying at a foster home and, around noon on a Sunday, had wandered off the grounds and into traffic – according to the Missing Person's report. By the time one of the other children had altered their caregiver, he'd been gone. He'd never been seen since except on that one snippet of security footage that his mother had identified him on, where he'd waited outside a tire and lube drop-off for forty-five minutes, eaten three protein bars that had been arranged in a basket for customers, then left again.

Xander considered the boy for a moment, then ripped out the top-left segment of the page with his name and photograph. He picked up the red sharpie at his feet and wrote 'FOSTER' on it in capital block letters, then worked a green pin from the palm of his hand to between his thumb and forefinger. He pinned Dylan's picture to the Diamond Springs subdivision he'd disappeared from, then stepped back until he could see the whole of the map again.

Becky Stephens had brown hair and hazel eyes. She was eight years old with freckles across her cheeks and a wide smile. She'd been last seen wearing a red dress with black trim when her father had picked her up from her mother's house for his weekly visit. The father's credit card was last used in Utah, but had since defaulted. There was an outstanding warrant for his arrest, and the girl was assumed alive.

Xander ripped Becky's photo out of her page and selected a red pin from his pack. He pressed her into the intersection of Corben and Hilliard where her mother lived, then stepped back again. This time he wrangled a cigarette out of his breast pocket and pressed it between his lips, his eyes going from Becky to Dylan to Luka's photographs. He'd almost had it lit when he stopped himself and looked back toward Crowley and Lisa's bedroom door.

He took the cigarette outside and smoked it all while leaning against his window and staring at the pile of paper he'd left.

When he returned, he picked up another sheet, almost at random. It was Cassandra Mitchell; she'd been eleven and had gone missing at a shopping center near Hollywood. She'd been out back-to-school shopping with her mother and had gone in to try on some clothes for size and never come back out.

Xander stared at her for a long moment, all back curls and braces, before sticking a yellow pin in her and affixing her to the map's approximation of Hollywood.

Julian Smith, twelve. Missing after a break-out at a juvenile detention center in Eastlake in which thirteen children had escaped during a fire. Twelve had been recovered in one way or another, but Julian hadn't been seen since. Yellow pin.

Ava Miller, eight. She'd been lured from her hotel while her parents were in town on a business trip. She'd wandered out of the hotel daycare with another girl about the same age who wasn't with the program, and had been last seen on a hotel camera near the pool. Green pin.

Jayden Martinez, ten. He and his younger sister were taken from their family home by their older brother, Fredrick Martinez, nineteen. Further investigation alluded to abuse and the Martinez parents were officially charged, with charges later dropped due to lack of evidence. The three Martinez children are suspected to have fled to Canada based on an eyewitness report at the border and in Calgary. Red pin. Xander found the file on the younger sister, Abigail, and pinned them both to the map with the same pin.

Camilla Jones, fourteen. Taken from a Willowbrook halfway house with signs of forced entry and some evidence of a struggle. In specific, nail filings against the frame of the door and a large clump of her hair that had been ripped out by the root had been found at the scene. She'd been seen three weeks later at a Wal-Mart trying to exchange an old DVD-player for money and looked to have lost thirty pounds on the footage.

Xander eyed Camilla's file image for a moment, then reached back into his pocket and withdrew the case of pins again. He singled out a purple pin and used it to affix the entire page to the Willowbrook suburb, without even cutting her photo out.

Nathan Moore, thirteen. Taken from a Quartz Hill Long-Term Care Facility with no evidence of wrongdoing, according to local police. Some had speculated an organized crime connection, but upon reading the article the officers involved suspected that purely on the youth's association with Quartz Hill, and Xander dismissed this. Nathan got a green pin.

Three youths had disappeared from Compton in a relatively short period of time, and Xander affixed them all alongside each other so that at least half their faces stuck out. The board was already getting crowded, and there were still many sheets of paper to run through.

"What's this?" Lisa asked, stepping up beside him. She was rubbing her eyes, and her tone said 'it is far too early for this' in volumes. She pressed the heels of both her palms into her eyes sockets as if she could make the images in front of her go away, let out a sigh, then removed them and opened her eyes comically wide.

"Migraine?" Xander asked, fidgeting and scratching at his side.

Lisa nodded. "Killer. Can't take codeine anymore either."

He nodded and took her hand. He pinched the webbing between her thumb and forefinger with deep, firm pressure, his eyes running from one child on the wall to the next as he did.

Crowley came out of her room wearing pink fuzzy pajamas, saw the both of them, then continued to the kitchen to turn on the coffee pot.

"You didn't answer," Lisa said, motioning toward the board.

Xander switched from one hand to the other. "Any better?"

She nodded, moving her head from side to side more freely than she had been a moment before.

Xander's gaze fell on Ava Miller, grinning back at him

from a school photo with a patchwork blue background. She was turned to her left and was looking over her shoulder at the camera, directly at Xander through the lens of time, smiling in a way that he suspected, wherever she was, that she wasn't right now. "They're missing children," he said finally, his voice hoarse when he did.

He felt an echo of gooseflesh travel up her arm.

Her eyes went from one to the other now, never lingering on one long before another caught her attention, then finally falling to the papers on the floor between them and the wall. "... All of them?"

Xander felt her pulse quicken through her hand. "Going back about a year, fitting certain criteria... yes."

"But... this isn't all of them. All of the missing kids."

"No."

"And this is... California?"

"Los Angeles. And the boroughs."

Crowley entered the living room with two cups of coffee and handed one of them to Lisa. "Decaf."

Lisa took it and nodded, taking a long swig without taking her eyes off the map on the wall.

Crowley drank some of her own, exiting the room and returning with a third cup and handing it to Xander. "Black."

He nodded and thanked her and they took a long slug of the thick brew together.

Lisa stepped forward away from the both of them, finally slipping her hand away from Xander's. Her migraine had returned in force and the pressure point massage was no longer helping. She stepped forward onto the scattered papers and bent down to look at them, then up at the wall of pinned pictures, and stepped close enough to delicately guide her hand along the pins.

"How'd you sleep?" Xander asked Crowley, the both of them watching as Lisa moved her hand from pin to pin.

"Not great, you?" Crowley replied.

"Not at all." He nodded at the stack of papers as if by way of explanation.

"What's with the pins?" Lisa asked, her thumb resting on the green pin for Nathan Moore.

"I'm trying to figure out which ones fit. According to Tim, there's been an uptick in disappearances, but it's not from nothing. Kids go missing. So it's a matter of figuring out which ones fit what we saw at LA Sun the best."

Lisa stepped back, looking at the green pins. "Green is sure? Yellow... not sure?"

"And red for doesn't fit."

Dylan Porter had a green pin and the word 'foster' written beneath his photo in red ink. Julian Smith, 'Juvie;' Nathan Moore, 'Orph', and Ava Miller, 'Hotel?'

Lisa looked at them and then squat down on the floor and picked up the closest piece of paper to her.

Crowley looked over the amassed papers and winced, turning back to Xander. "I'm going out. I have an appointment... do we need anything?"

"Some hot water bottles for Lisa, maybe. Helps with the migraines."

She nodded. "Any food?"

He shook his head.

She touched his arm. "You good for smokes?"

He winced. "Yes, I'm good... Don't get me those.

Lisa?"

"Orange Juice," Lisa mumbled, as she read down the page with a hand hovering just adjacent to her lips. "Going through it like candy."

Crowley nodded, then took her coffee back to the kitchen and took off her slippers. "Have a good day?"

"You too," Xander and Lisa said, almost in unison. He squat down and picked up a sheet of paper and started to read its description of the disappearance.

"Greta Myers, age ten. Taken from a short-term facility near Quartz Hill," Lisa said, holding up the page.

"Green pin," Xander said, taking the pack of pins out of his pocket and tossing them to her. "Mark it."

She nodded, ripping Greta's picture out of the sheet with great care.

Fifteen minutes later, Crowley came out of her room ready to go out, and the two had kept their positions, with the only difference being that the amount of children pinned to the wall had doubled.

CHAPTER EIGHT

There were two windows open on Tim White's computer, each one occupying half of the screen. The window on the right was split horizontally, with the upper half being a family tree of known associates of Stephen Fields and the lower half a list of employees that had worked for the Long-and-Short-Term Care facilities in LA in the last twelve months. Tim was slowly going through them and updating close friends and acquaintances, looking for commonalities between the Fields list and the Care-Worker list. So far there had been one, a respite worker whose brother had low-level connections to one of Fields' lieutenants.

The second window was open to a video of a young woman looking at him through the camera lens. She was smiling and holding a hairbrush up and stroking it over the field of vision and whispering softly as she did. The caption of the video that scrolled across read: ASMR Role-play – Salon.

ASMR stood for Autonomous Sensory Meridian Response and was a form of auditory-tactile synaesthesia that Tim had discovered since his paralysis. In ASMR videos, the artist attempted to induce this synaesthesia into the viewer with mainly auditory, but some visual, cues. In the small segment of the population that experienced the effect, it was described as "pleasant tingling" or "gooseflesh."

Since his injury, Tim had discovered it was the only way he could simulate feeling in his upper arm. The best of the ASMRtists, as they preferred to be called, could simulate the feeling of being touched through auditory manipulation. In moments of hyper-focused listening, Tim could feel the shudder of the tingles shoot up and down his limbs, even though he knew intellectually that it was all in his head.

The woman on the screen brought her scissors up to the camera and pretended to snip the hair of the viewer, laying her hand on the shoulder for support. It didn't matter that she was actually laying her hand on a piece of fabric next to a microphone – the effect was the same, the illusion of tactile contact.

On the right-hand screen Tim pulled up the FBI file on a man named Albert Venture, a name that simply oozed of pseudonym. The picture that came up was one of a middle-aged man with receding hair and a bright, happy, open-mouthed smile. His teeth were tiny round nubs, worn down to useless safety-scissor versions of their former selves.

When Albert had been twenty, he had been implicated in human trafficking involving minors. He had been working for a pizzeria in the downtown area, one of those buildings that had once been a multiple-storey home and now the first floor was a restaurant and the upper floors were used for storage; only in this instance they weren't used for storage, they were used for filming and storing short promotional videos of the children that were available for purchase. Reports had even alleged that the building had been used to store some of the children as well, but those charges had never been borne out. The on-file notes on the case indicated that investigating agents had suspected Albert of being more than a hapless young adult who'd worked at the wrong street-meat pizzeria; they'd suspected that he had been equal parts cameraman and caretaker for the children above the pizzeria.

Despite this suspicion and multiple charges laid against others in the organization, there hadn't been enough physical or eyewitness evidence to have charged Albert with anything. He left the pizzeria in disgust over what had been going on under his nose before it had to be closed down and used the circumstances surrounding his departure to secure unemployment wages for well over a year. Since then he'd moved from job to job, staying longest at an 'As-Seen-On-TV' kiosk at a local mall, a position he'd held for three months. Even with his high turnover rate, he had managed to work for twelve different organizations related to child care in the last ten years, none of them for longer than ninety days at a time.

The girl on the video moved out of frame and started to make sounds as though she were around the back of Tim's head.

There was a heavy knock at the door.

Tim jolted mentally, and was equal parts relieved and annoyed that he had not actually moved. He pressed a speaker icon on his desktop and a third window expanded, a cartoon grill-style microphone speaker and two buttons, one green and one red. He pressed the green and then spoke. "Hello?"

There was a sound from the speaker like shuffling, and a lot of static.

He pressed the button again. "If you speak, I can hear you."

"Looking for Tim White's place," came the return voice, though it was faint. Tim had experienced this before: the user was looking around to find a camera to look into and finding none. Even so there was an unmistakeable drawl to the way the person said the name *Tim*, with the 'I' sound just a little too long and becoming nasally.

Tim winced and hovered his curser over the red button, let it sit there for a moment, then sighed and returned it to the green and double-clicked it. He heard the telltale electronic buzz of his front door's lock disengaging, and then of the door opening. It was a sound he was used to hearing when he'd worked in small towns and was buzzed into convenience stores that he responded to break-ins at.

Tim closed the intercom and opened the live feed of his camera in time to see Duncan Taggart enter his living room, his shoes still on and tracking in gravel.

Duncan stopped just at the edge of where the scant hallways opened into the main room and was looking at Tim's elaborate setup, sitting upright in an electronically controlled bed with screens surrounding him. He'd stopped and had lost some of his colour when he saw it, as though he were reconsidering something fundamental. He hadn't noticed the camera lens pointed at him yet, and was unaware that Tim could see him.

"Come in, Duncan," Tim said gruffly, his eyes twitching from the video feed to the list with Albert Venture on it, annoyed that he wasn't getting any further down it.

Duncan swallowed, steeled himself, then took a step forward until he was able to meet Tim's eye for what he thought was the first time. "Afternoon," he said, his voice a small thing in the back of his throat.

Tim squinted. "Hello, Duncan."

Duncan twitched, then turned despite his best effort and looked down the bed along the arc of the sheet that covered Tim's lower half. When his gaze reached his feet, he sucked in air through pursed lips as though he'd been holding it in, then his head snapped back, suddenly aware of its own motion. "Jesus Christ, they really took a piece out of you, didn't they, White?" He spoke in the hushed, reverent tone of someone who'd thought they'd had a grasp of a reality only to be confronted with it.

Tim's lip curled at the way Duncan said his name.

"I'm sorry I didn't come into town or call or anything when... when it happened," Duncan said, still shaken. He looked as though he had to physically restrain himself from looking down the bed: Tim's legs were crossed at an awkward angle, but Tim had not noticed.

"Is there something I can help you with?"

Duncan stiffened. "There have been murders. At the Shane company... I've been brought in to work it."

"Probation over, is it?"

"Oh, fuck you," Duncan snarled. He pushed Tim's screen back a smidge. "I'm trying to do good here, but I don't..." he shuffled, then fidgeted with his coat. "... I don't do West Coast well. This city, this... everything. It gets to you, gets under your skin. I swear, I think I've lost two pounds since I came here, no joke." He forced himself to meet Tim's eye. "I need help on this. I need a sounding board."

"I've got my own caseload at the moment. Despite what you might think, I've been keeping busy."

"Four dead," Duncan said, flatly. "Don't turn this into a me-and-you thing... four dead."

Tim frowned, his gaze turning back to the window with the list of Fields suspects on his screen. Albert Venture's face was peeking out at him from behind the window he'd opened to speak to Duncan.

"Fine, I get it." Duncan sighed and turned to walk out. He tried to think of something to else to say before he left, but couldn't.

When he heard the sound of his front latch connect, Tim closed the intercom app and went back to his research.

There was tea in front of Crowley despite the morning. It had come from an instant coffee pod and was called London Fog and had a muddy, white, sinewy texture that repulsed Crowley as she looked into it. The colour and texture reminded her of rendered fat and semen, and the thought of putting the hot mug filled with it anywhere near her face made her lips curl.

"How'd you sleep?" Susan asked. She jotted down the time from the clock in the upper right hand corner of her page.

Crowley turned from the London Fog to Susan, the

scowl remaining intact. "Does that ever work?"

She smiled a practiced smile. "I find that first night after the intake people lie in bed and think of all the things they want to talk about, things they should say, things they should have said… you know 'I used to smoke, should I have put down that I'm a smoker? Is it asking if I am currently, or if I ever have been?' Things like that."

Crowley nodded.

Susan made a note. "So, tell me about this guy."

Crowley smiled slightly, looked as though she were about to speak, then stopped herself.

"It's all confidential."

She smiled again, more wanly. "Xander is…" She thought back to him the way he'd looked this morning, standing in their living room surrounded by papers, the map of Los Angeles poorly pinned to the wall across from him. His right index and middle fingers had been flicking back and forth at his side in a way she wasn't sure he was aware of, as if he were flipping through files in his head. She'd noted him doing it three times now, each time when he was deep in thought. "… Driven," she finished after a pregnant pause.

Susan made a note, but didn't speak.

"The way he makes decisions is incredible to me. He can make these huge choices that are like, life and death, so quickly, like: no fuck's given. But he does give a fuck, you know what I mean? Like, if I really gave a fuck about something like he does, it'd take me all day to make a choice on it, but he can just make the choice and then deal with it if it goes to shit, and I don't even think he thinks about the choice if it does go to shit."

Susan nodded again, smiling. "What does he do?"

Crowley opened her mouth, then paused.

"Again, confidential."

"He's a detective," she answered finally, after some hesitation.

"Oh, wow," Susan smiled, making a note and circling it. "I imagine a lot of that decisiveness rubs off from his job, then."

Crowley tilted her head and closed one eye, pantomiming thought. "I'm not sure he's ever *not* working, actually. Like I said, driven."

Susan made a note. "Anything else?"

There was a long pause. "… he can compartmentalize. He's like me, like that. Like, he can joke and be funny, but then when something comes up about a case, it's like a switch, he can just turn it off: business now, all business."

"Is this a positive or a negative, you think?"

"Positive. Definitely."

Susan nodded. "I tend to agree."

Lisa stared at the map that was pinned to her living room wall, invading her quiet space with hundreds of tiny pin-pricked holes. The map was still pinned haphazardly at its corners, but no longer needed it: the amount of push-pins in it now would have kept it upright and against the wall by themselves.

There were dozens of pins, posting the images of missing children to every square inch of Los Angeles: from Beverly Hills to Compton, and everywhere in between.

She'd seen reports about some of them: on a news bulletin in the background at work or on an Amber Alert ad on the bus during her morning commute... but to see them all like this, at once, clustered around each other was different. To see them all together focused her awe and her rage, and it made them all come together as one singular unit. They were all different: European, African, Asian, Middle-Eastern, Mexican... but they were all children, and they all smiled back at her in classroom and family photos with the same chubby-cheeked smile that said the same thing: once, I was happy.

Xander squat beside her, crouched on the balls of his feet in a way she was beginning to suspect he found comfortable, but couldn't imagine being such. His elbows were rested on his knees and his hands came together to form a triangle that cupped his nose and chin together. He was still but his eyes darted from one end of the map to the other, fluttering around his sockets like someone in REM sleep. They would focus on one child, briefly, then get distracted by another.

Los Angeles was a sea of red pins, so many that some double up in high-risk areas. Next to that were yellow pins, spread sporadically throughout the map. There were fewer green pins, but still an alarming amount, in small clusters around different areas of the map, usually intermingled with beads of yellow as well. There were five large clusters and several smaller ones, and only two green pins were completely alone... so much so that Xander contemplated changing them to yellow chiefly because of their anomalous nature.

The floor was clear of papers. When they'd gotten

down to their last dozen and Xander was having a hard time placing them, Lisa had taken the discarded scraps the photos had been ripped from and stacked them in the corner along with the file folders they'd originally come in. The last pin had been pushed in twenty minutes ago, and they'd both stepped back to see what they'd done as if only seeing it as a whole at that moment, and neither had spoken since.

Xander sighed deeply, then stood and walked over to the map. He wrapped his index and middle fingers around a red pin affixing Andre Michaels to the wall and pulled it out, palming the pin but letting the picture flutter to the floor.

"What're you doing?" Lisa asked, holding both arms up.

Xander pulled another red pin out to the same affect, then stepped back and used its tip to point at the different areas of the map. "Green is for those we think are involved with the case, kids that went missing from care facilities or with other kids or whatever. Yellow we aren't sure about, red we're pretty sure didn't."

"Yeah?"

"We're colour blind," he said, motioning to the whole map. "Red-Green colour blind. We're supposed to be looking at the green pins, but we can't help but look at them all, because they're all kids. It's understandable... it's not helpful."

She swallowed, then nodded, but did not help him take down the clippings.

He removed three in one motion, the red pallops of plastic fitting in the gaps between his fingers. He hesitated over the full-page posting of Camilla Jones, then pulled it out by its purple pin. He did not let the page fall to the floor though, he pinned it to the wall opposite the map and then resumed removing the red pins.

As the floor started to fill with papers again, Lisa turned and walked into the kitchen to get some toast.

When all the red pins had been removed, he collected the papers into a neat stack and added them to the pile she'd made in the corner, laying the pins on top of them in a cluttered pile of metal and plastic. He stepped back, zooming out until he could see the entire wall, now a heavily perforated map of Los Angeles with clusters of green and yellow, with some yellow scattered throughout and very few lone green pins.

He backed up until Lisa saw him from the kitchen, and she rejoined him. She stood next to him and stared at the map with five green clusters on it.

Xander squinted. "I could use some help here."

She turned to him, surprised. "Pardon?"

He pursed his lips. There was a long silence as he appeared to gather his thoughts. She could almost see the gears inside his head working. "I'm at my best when there's something to hit... even if I'm not thinking with my fists, I'm better when there's a direct target. Something to focus on... with kids it's different, it's so hard to focus on the target because you focus on the victim, because how can you not, and it all gets... muddled."

Her brow curled upward. She turned from Xander to the wall, and then back again.

"I don't have a great track record for dealing with missing kids. It's not... it's not my strong suit. I'm good at dead victims – when the victim is already dead, there's only so much damage you can do when trying to find the fucker what did it."

She nodded.

"This," he waved a hand toward the map. "This I could fuck up."

She ate the last of her toast staring at the wall. "We need to get rid of the yellows," she said with finality.

"Can't. Don't know which are which."

"No, exactly." She stepped over closer to the walls. "Those are what we need to be looking at. We need to look at the yellows in the middle of these green clusters" she motioned to them with circular gestures "and make them green, or make them red and remove them." She motioned to the lone green and yellow pins, apart from the five main clusters. "And we need to check on these. These yellows, are they really reds? Then get rid of them. Are those greens really green? Then maybe we can learn a lot from those... because they're away from the rest? Like, what makes them so special?"

Xander nodded. "Even then, it's not organized like Fields, but it's not random like when they're taken by family..." he motioned to each cluster in kind, each of them centered around a care facility. There were between six and eight pins at each, these tiny little clusters of missing children. "It's so evenly spaced. So... organized. But nothing so organized would risk using other kids for the get. And there's nothing..." he motioned to the entire map. "There's nothing the *same*. Nothing jumping out at me."

Lisa looked at the children again, each of them different. She pulled back until she was on parity with Xander again, then stepped into the kitchen to get some tea.

Tim read through his file on Roberto Raid as one of the workers he employed vacuumed around him. He didn't find it distracting, in fact he felt the white noise helped: it drowned out the sounds of the house that he could otherwise do nothing to investigate, and made him calmer. He'd priced a white noise generator on Amazon twice now, but had yet to pull the trigger in ordering a device that made a noise most people would find irritating.

Raid had a long and sordid criminal history. When added up, the fifty-year old had spent twenty-eight of the last thirty years in prison for a wide variety of crimes from arms dealing to abduction to manslaughter to conspiracy. Since he'd been eighteen (and possibly before, Tim had yet to attempt to pull his juvenile records), he had only been out of prison a maximum of two months at a time before being arrested again and awaiting trial. On the surface he seemed like someone who a man like Stephen Fields would stay far away from... but he'd been caught on camera each time he'd been freed at a bank which was known to have been used by Fields. Tim had the security footage of the most recent of those visits on his screen now, a blurry shot taken three years ago.

Behind the window showing Raid's profile, and the window with the list comparing Fields employees to careworkers in the Los Angeles area, and the window with the intercom application, was the window with the notes he had written to go over with Xander during their barbeque. The window peeked out from around the rest and popped up to remind him of its presence every time he alt-tabbed between screens.

The top line of the document was still visible, the one that started with the known information on Rae Stevens, the Shane employee who was killed on Nordoff Street.

Tim eyed it for a long moment... then sighed, saved his file on Raid, and tabbed the file on Rae Stevens to the front of his pile and started to read, the drone of the vacuum in the distance drowning out anything else.

Crowley put three gallon bottles of orange juice in the fridge: one in the door and two in the body. She reached back into the reusable shopping bag she'd pulled them out of and withdrew two bottles of jam – apricot and mixed berry blend – and placed them both in the door of the fridge as well.

She reached in once more and withdrew an unopened pack of Camel cigarettes. She unwrapped the cellophane from it and took out the paper insert within, then opened the cupboard door and removed the nearly-empty pack from there, then replaced it with this new pack. She craned her head to make sure nobody was watching, pocketed the pack with only two cigarettes left in it, then put the rest of the groceries away.

She bridged the gap between the kitchen and the living room and saw Xander and Lisa standing near the map on the far wall. Both of them were regarding a single yellow pin between them with great interest. "Have you guys been at that all day?"

Lisa turned, then nodded. She sat on the floor where

she had been standing, as if Crowley had reminded her that she could do such a thing, then put the laptop in the middle of her crossed legs and started to read.

Xander stayed where he had been, stroking the outline of his mouth with his thumb and forefinger.

The yellow pin was in the middle of a cul-de-sac in West Hollywood, and was far removed from any of the other clusters of green and yellow pins Crowley saw. The red pins were gone, as were the pieces of paper that had been attached to them. She stepped forward until she was between the both of them, still a few steps further away from the map than they were.

"Get anywhere with it?" she asked him. She was aimed at him, her shoulder facing Lisa.

His mouth twitched, his lip curling slightly. "Not as far as I'd like," he said ruefully. "How was your day?"

"Good," she said reflexively, then stopped to think of it for a moment, and nodded. "Yeah, *good*. Not great, but... you know."

He nodded.

"Listen," she started, and felt her hand clasp the same frill at the end of her shirt. "I was wondering about breakfast tomorrow."

Lisa's head raised slowly from the screen and turned to face the conversation she was overhearing.

"We have eggs, I think," Xander said, looking over the streets that fed into the offending cul-de-sac. "No bacon, unless you picked some up. And waffles, waffles are always good."

"I was more thinking about going out to eat?"

Lisa closed the laptop and stood up slowly, bracing

herself against the wall to account for her odd center of gravity. She left the room quietly, trying not to draw attention to herself.

"Yeah," Xander said, raising his eyebrows. "Yeah, there's a few good places around; although I'd walk about five blocks before eating anything. This isn't a part of town known for its A-plus restaurants."

She frowned and stopped herself from rolling the edge of her shirt around her thumbs. "No." She took a deep breath and steadied herself. "I'm asking if you'd like to go to breakfast with me."

Xander stopped, then turned to look at her, diverting his attention away from the map for the first time since she'd come in. He realized only then how close they were to one another, as close as they'd been the other night after the barbeque. They were less than a foot apart and he realized with sudden, ecstatic discomfort that he could smell the body wash she used all around him, their proximity wafting it in clouds around him like waves.

"Of course," he nodded, looking at her. He stepped away from the map. "I mean... Of course. That'd be great."

"Great," she smiled.

"There's a spot on Cliffton Avenue that's nice. It's got some --"

"Yeah," she smiled, showing her teeth. "I mean, wherever is great. I'm not so much caring where we eat."

There was a sound from the kitchen as Lisa hit her knee off the open cupboard and cursed.

"Yes," Xander nodded, motioning from the map to Crowley and back again. "*Yes.* Breakfast is good, it'll be...

good. I'll do this some more and then tomorrow, breakfast. That's okay?"

She nodded, then turned and walked back into the
kitchen.

He found himself watching her until she was out of
sight before he could draw his gaze back to the problem
of the yellow pins on the map.

CHAPTER NINE

Desmond Hart was sitting alone in the community room at the far end of the Sommerfield Youth Care Center. It was a large, open space that ran along the western edge of the building, sharing a wall with the dining room, the kitchen, the main hall, and the chapel. The chapel hadn't been in use since Sommerfield had gone public, but people still called it that. The cross had been taken out and replaced by a whiteboard and the pews had been replaced with desks, but it still had the architecture of a chapel: that upside down boat look that seemed to have been the blueprint for all places of worship for the better part of a century.

The community room was one long room that went the entire length of the building on the west side, and looked out onto the backyard. It was so long that it was divided into three sections, not by walls but by seat arrangements: three chairs were arranged around the fireplace at one end, another four around a bookcase packed with novels and board games, and near the far wall was a table with four chairs around it.

Desmond was sitting in the middle of the three areas, lying down across the couch with his neck and shoulders popped up by one arm. His feet were up, something the Organizers would have hated him doing... but they weren't here and he didn't think they were anywhere close by, so his feet went up. He was playing a worn Nintendo DS that had had its case chipped and cracked in places. Someone, at some point, had bought a device from overseas that allowed one to download any game and insert it into the handheld with an SD card, so now Desmond was playing Super Metroid on his DS Lite without having the slightest inkling as to what an accomplishment that would have been to anyone who had grown up during the golden age of gaming. All he knew was that the atmospheric tones and chimes of the classic soundtrack didn't sound quite right coming out of the tiny speakers, sounding tinny and shrill.

He'd been at Sommerfield for over a month, since just after his fourteenth birthday. His parents had taken a trip to Atlantic City without him and he'd been fine at first, but after a week had found it difficult to get up and go to school in the morning, often missing the bus and then considering the day a lost cause. After three weeks of bad attendance and ignored calls, texts, and emails to his parents, the administrative staff at his school had called in social services, who had intervened and discovered that Desmond was, in fact, living alone. The LAPD (Los Angeles Police Department) had put out an APB (All Points Bulletin) for his ALPs (At Large Parents), but as of yet they hadn't shown up on the radar of anyone who watched such things for a living. When asked where they might be if not in Atlantic City, Desmond had suggested that the police try Vegas instead.

He liked it at Sommerfield for the most part. He had a hard time with the administrative staff (having lived on his own for weeks and been virtually on his own for years prior, he detested now being told what to do and when to do it again) and was having trouble adjusting to the routine of the scheduling again, but other than that he was adjusting fine. He liked his room: he had his own room here, and although it was tiny, it had its own sink. The novelty of that had impressed him. He liked the other wards here: it was a coed facility, and there was a girl named Brittany that he fancied quite well, although he hadn't gotten up the courage yet to talk to her except in large group discussions. She was a year older than him but a foot shorter, and he found himself paying more attention in subjects that she excelled in the most, if only to have something he might talk to her about.

The only thing he didn't like about Sommerfield was the *church*.

It wasn't a church anymore it was a classroom, but it was still a church. As far as Desmond was concerned, church was something you couldn't make go away just by taking out the cross and replacing the pews. Church was something that came out of the people who attended like sweat and was absorbed by the walls of a room, making the boards thick with it. Church got into the paint and made the carpet damp. Church was a smell that every church he'd ever been in had and that the classroom had too; and so it *wasn't* a classroom, it was a *church*.

He hadn't liked churches for as long as he could remember. If he was pressed he would say that he hadn't liked churches since he was four years old, although he had a hard time pinning down exactly *why* he chose this age, when pressed. Memories from that time existed in an ephemeral fog that only lifted in rare moments of extreme concentration or extreme relaxation, and Desmond didn't typically have time for either. He enjoyed relaxing far too much to concentrate, and he had too much to concentrate on to relax, so the memories remained adrift amidst the clouds of water-vapor in his mind.

There was a sound from out in the hallway, the long creak of a floorboard that his ears had become attuned to over the last month. He took his feet down off the couch and turned to look over its back, out through the door that led into the main hallway.

There was nothing except a copy of Lord of the Rings Risk that had been wedged next to the doorway, rather than packed away neatly with the rest of the games on the bottom floor of the bookshelf.

Desmond turned down the volume on his game, and listened.

There was usually some noise in Sommerfield. There were too many people, both staff and wards, and the building was too old, for there not to be. Pipes made sounds, floorboards made sounds, the walls made sounds when the weather got hot and again when it got cold. The air conditioners made sounds and the carpet fibres made sounds when the air conditioner's breeze fell on them. Right now though, with the volume on Super Metroid turned down to mute and his breath held and his ears perked, Sommerfield seemed to be completely silent.

Brittney walked past the door, so quietly that he almost jumped out of his skin. "Jesus," he said, and some part of him that had been raised not to say that word in that context chided himself.

She jumped as well, turning as if she were going to strike at him from across the room, a cat on a hot tin roof. "Fuck," she breathed. Curses never sounded right coming out of that mouth. She had one of those voices that was too high-pitched for dirty language. It sounded weird, like a child playing with adult speech in a play.

"What are you doing u—" he stopped half way through the question when another youth, one he did not recognize, appeared in the door behind Brittney. A male youth. "Who's that?"

The new boy looked around the community room and then stepped in. He swaggered over to rest against the back of the chair Desmond was sitting on, then leaned in, turning his head to look from one end of the room to the other and make sure no one was there.

Brittney came in behind him, stepping much more tentatively. Now that she was in the bright fluorescent light of the community room, Desmond could see that she was pale, her skin almost paper white except for her freckles, and her red bangs clutched to her forehead with a thin coat of nervous sweat. She had her backpack, and was holding both straps at the shoulders with the thumb of each hand. Her eyes fluttered about the room, as if expecting one of the staff to come out from behind one of the couches at any moment.

The boy leaned on the back of the couch, his ear-length blonde hair toppling forward. He smiled at Desmond. "My name is Mark," he said, extending his hand and a broad, welcoming smile. His cheeks were bony and looked like they could have cut Desmond's flesh if he got close enough, and although the smile seemed genuine, the dark rings of malnourishment under each of his eyes left something resembling suspicion in the pit of Desmond's stomach.

That, and the smell that came off the boy. He smelled like cigarettes and his mouth smelled like rot even though his teeth looked perfect, and his clothes smelled like *church*. That smell, that same antiseptic stained-wood smell that no amount of scrubbing could get out of the walls and carpets of their classroom was all over this boy named Mark.

Chelsea Robbins sat behind her desk, the blueish-green tint of her computer screen washing over her in the low light of the room and bathing her in the jade hue. Although she had been sitting behind her desk for the last three hours, she hadn't typed anything for the last thirty minutes. Instead she was rubbing the cartilage between the thumb and forefinger of her left hand with her right knuckle, with such vigor and intensity that it had gone numb and turned red. She was on day three of a five day Juice Cleanse, was fighting a migraine so intense that it sent shockwaves through her skull with every beat of her heart, and refused to undo her progress by introducing any more toxic acetaminophen into her system.

On the screen in front of her was an Excel spreadsheet displaying lines 1270 to 1283 of a five thousand line document. The only other application open was a word processing app, which until thirty minutes ago she had been tabbing back and forth between to add insight to the data she was analyzing for a presentation to the partners three Mondays from now. The presentation was on account points of contact, how many times a corporate client had to call their support staff for assistance, and the attrition rate thereafter. It was long work, it was boring work, and it was work one could only do well if they had the sort of personality that was prone to hyper-focalization.

Chelsea was this person. She ran spreadsheets and reported on them; that was what Chelsea did. She had no aspirations of moving up the corporate ladder, she only wanted one thing: to be good enough at her job that it remained stable, and to be left alone to do it. As such, she had accepted only lateral career shifts, never promotions that would have taken her away from long sheets of numbers and data and graphs. She could spend hours reading and typing impressions and bullet points and collating into charts with a podcast or soundtrack blaring through her bone-conduction glasses that she'd bought special, adding her prescription lenses after the fact.

She could become so hyper-focused that she could look up even after hours of typing and data management, and realize that the large open concept office she worked out of was completely empty, which she did right now as she finally gave up the rhythmic rubbing of her thumb and stood to ask Katrina if she had any Advil, only to find the room deserted.

She stood in shock for a moment, perplexed by her surroundings being different than what she had anticipated – like when you went into a movie during daylight and came out in the black of night. It wasn't a jarring change or a substantial shock, but it was enough to surprise some part of your limbic brain that liked time and disliked being fooled by it.

Still, it wasn't the first time it had happened and the disorientation faded quickly with a curse and a glance at the clock. She put her purse over her shoulder and made her way out to the hallway.

The daytime lights in the hall were off as well, with only one in every five remaining on, and those were dimmed. The effects were islands of light that made the floor seem like pools of inky black. There was a long row of vending machines along the right wall that was veiled in shadow, and as she walked towards them, she heard the soles of her shoes clip and clap against the linoleum. Was there something about the dark that made sharp sounds echo more? She thought so, but had failed to look it up any time she'd tried. They always led her down the Wikipedia rabbit-hole to articles with sciences and terms she had trouble understanding, that required base knowledge she didn't have, and before she knew it hours had gone by and she was no closer to finding an answer.

There were three vending machines and a water bottle refill station all in a row in the dark nether-realm between two sets of night lights. One was filled with chips and chocolates, another with sealed ready-made sandwiches, and the third with cold drinks. The machine with the chips and chocolate bars had a bottom row reserved for cough drops, nasal sprays, and pain relievers.

She fished a payment card out of her breast pocket, took three attempts to slide it into the paper-thin card slot, then pressed J7, and waited as the pill bottle dispensed itself. Her headache must be getting worse, because the metal spring that clutched the bottle seemed to move unbearably slowly, and the gnashing of the gears that made it move felt like they were scraping the inside of her skull.

She picked the bottle out of the receptacle and opened it immediately, shaking out two pills and dry-swallowing them both where she stood. She took out a third, put it in her mouth, then walked to the water bottle station and released some water into her cupped hand, then used it to swallow. The pills went down hard; even the act of putting her head back making the back of her head squelch at its joint.

Far on the other end of the hall, opposite from where she'd come, came two sharp snaps followed by a static hum.

The sound cut through her throbbing head like a knife, and she wasn't sure if the hum was really there or if it was her achy head's reaction to the sound. She turned off the faucet.

"Hello?" she called out, her voice echoing off the sterile walls all the way down the hall.

The hum stuttered twice, then resumed. It was an electronic hum, the type heard when one's television was tuned to a feed with no input: the blue screen hum, the television's idea of silence.

Her eyes scanned the hallway for the source of the sound, but found nothing. She expected there to be light: the spark of an exposed crop of wire, or a faulty outlet, and she'd have to call up security to deal with it. But there was no visual clue to go along with this new sound that hadn't been there a few minutes before – there was only the hum.

"Is anyone there?" she called again, and started down the hallway towards the source.

Mark sat on the edge of the walkway with a cigarette clasped between his thumb and forefinger. It looked un-natural, the way a child trying smoking for the first time held a cigarette. He was staring at Desmond, who was standing on the street before, at eye height.

"You from South side?" Mark asked, punctuating the question by tapping the ash.

Desmond squinted at him, but did not respond. He turned instead to Brittney, who was lingering several feet away at the mouth of the alley that divided Sommerfield from the pastry shop next door.

She was staring down the narrow gap of the alley as though she could see in the dark, her thumbs riding the sharp bones of her cheeks in a way he knew she only did when she was nervous. Her feet were swerving, as though she were drunk and trying desperately to stay in place.

"What's up?" Desmond asked, as he stepped up be-hind her. She jolted slightly from the sound even though he'd made no effort to conceal his approach. He peered over her shoulder into the deep black, accented only by the reflection of ambient light off the smog. There were square, geometric shapes kissed by the light here and there, only their outlines visible. One was an old garbage dumb, the type with hinged doors they didn't use any-more, another more vertical rectangle that must have been the fire escape, and far above that was the window that led into Brittney's floor. That was how Mark had gotten in without him seeing him, Desmond decided.

From this proximity, he could also see that Brittney was shaking. "Hey, what's wrong?" Desmond said softly, placing a rough-hewn palm on either of her shoulders. She was covered in gooseflesh.

"Y-y-y-y—" she stammered, as though they were in the frigid cold of the Arctic instead of a humid Los Angeles street. "You don't see it?" When she spoke she didn't turn to him, didn't blink, didn't do anything that would take her eyes off of the shapes in the alleyway.

Mark stood and straightened his shirt, his cigarette clasped between pursed lips.

Desmond turned to the alley and tried to focus, but the light from the city made it hard to see anything but blackness. "See what?" he whispered. "What's there?"

"We should get going," Mark called out to neither of them in particular, although both of them turned at the sound of his voice. It was a proclamation, like a troubadour at a stand window. "We don't want to be late."

Desmond nodded and stepped away, taking Brittney's hand. He'd thought of doing that several times before, and this time did it without contemplation. She didn't move until her hand was fully extended and he forced he to, and even then she could not tear her eyes away from the alley until the siding of Sommerfield finally obstructed her gaze.

▼

Chelsea had followed the source at the humming through two turns of the hallway, and was now finally staring straight up at its source. It was a camera just outside of the floor's midsized boardroom, and from her current vantage point it was staring directly at her.

The sound it made was blisteringly loud, the sort of highly-intense white noise that made one's skin crawl and itch with imaginary insects. It had switched three times while she'd been searching for it, turning from the blue-screen hum she'd gone searching for to that no-signal static she'd heard best described as a Snow Crash. Now both sounds were coming out of the camera at the same time, intermittently stopping and starting again, but never with both off at once.

She didn't think cameras like that even had speakers, so she couldn't imagine what was happening internally with the mechanics to force it to make such sounds.

She patted her pockets for her phone and did not find it. Sighing, she eyed the cord connecting the camera to its power outlet. She looked around, saw nothing nearby that would help her, then eventually started to work off her shoe.

The sound was sputtering now, and she was worried that that meant something unpleasant was on the verge of happening. She drew back and tossed her shoe at the camera's power cord, hitting the wall alongside it and making a small dent before clamoring to the floor.

"Fuck," she snapped, unable to hear even her own voice over the buzzing, static scream. She stepped forward, found her show in the near dark, then stepped back into position. She drew back again, took a steadying moment, then let the moderately priced footwear sail through the air.

It connected with the plug just right, dislodging it from the back of the camera. The screeching hum stopped immediately.

There was a deep, shuddering breath down the hall from where she'd come.

She turned so quickly her hair whipped at her cheeks, a small sound escaping her lips that her ears were ringing too much to register.

The islands of light created by the night illumination of the building seem to go on forever, spotlights for unseen dancers getting small and smaller in the dark until the bled into one continuous line. There was nary a soul in either of them, each beam as unoccupied as they'd been before she'd stepped through them.

"Hello?" she called out, her accent taking grip on her larynx in that moment of fear.

As she watched, the spotlights continued to float there, dangling in the darkness as if suspended there by strings.

A man stepped through one of the lights, its harsh glow covering him in shadow, before he disappeared into the darkness between the beams again.

She gasped and stepped back a pace, her hand cupping at her mouth without her even realizing it.

"Who's there?" she called out into the spotted dark, hearing her voice echo off of the nothingness of the halls.

He stepped into the light again, much closer now: he had not appeared at the next spotlight, but had skipped five and was now halfway to her.

His hair was fierce and unkempt, jutting out at random intervals and meeting with the sandpaper scruff that lined his chin, catching the light above and making long shadows against his hallowed cheeks with it. He seemed tall in the spotlight, as though it drew him out somehow, elongating him. His muscles were taut and defined, the veins in his arm pulsing with every step he took towards her. His shirt was tight and black and featureless, his pants the sort of tight black denim that was hard to move in, although he seemed to have no issues with momentum.

His jaw was set and his eyes were in shadow, cast from the light off of his looming, thick brow. Despite all logic, Chelsea would have still sworn that she could tell they were trained directly onto her.

The strange man disappeared into the darkness at the end of the spotlight again.

Chelsea found herself stepping away from the direction the man was coming from, backing up without even thinking about it, some long-dormant mammalian instinct sparking to life and forcing her legs to move, a hypnagogic kick without the cumbersome fact of being horizontal.

When she tried to put pressure on her left foot, she misjudged where the floor was without her shoe, slipped, and fell to the hard linoleum against her tailbone. She heard it crack against the walls, the echo of it snapping out like a sonic boom.

He appeared in the light again, even closer than he had been: within twenty feet of her. He was so close now that she could see his eyes despite the harsh light, and how they were trained on her, their whites bloodshot to the point of being pink. Blood blisters dotted his right forearm, and in his hand was a long, sharp blade that caught the light and brought it back up into his rough-hewn face.

Chelsea screamed, scrambled to her feet, and ran.

Brittney was shaking, leaning against the sheet metal of a large plastic clown. The three of them were standing in the driveway of a closed fast-food restaurant that had clearly attempted to set itself up as a franchise and failed to make a return on investment, the rusted hollow husk of the clown statue that served as the intercom's speaker a monument to that failure. She was huddled under the speaker box with her legs curled up to her chin, her arms wrapped around her legs, and her eyes glued to some invisible spot on the ground three feet away.

Desmond squatted a few feet from her in the fake plastic grass that surrounded the intercom. It was a bright green that was too bright, attempting to look inviting but stretching itself into the uncanny valley colour of a bad acid trip. He had tried to reach out and touch her knee twice to comfort her, but the sound she'd made had made him draw back.

Mark was behind them, standing on the yellow line directly in the center of the drive-through lane. He was smoking a cigarette again; had, in fact, been chain-smoking them ever since they had left Sommerfield, lighting the new one off the embers of the old.

"What's wrong with her?" Desmond snapped, turning over his shoulder to glare at Mark. It was not the first time he had asked the question in a way that accused Mark since they'd left, and each time the accusation carried more and more venom on it.

Mark took a drag from his cigarette, the embers illuminating his face in orange. For a moment he was a Jack-O-Lantern, his angular features carved from his gaunt skull

"What did you do to her?" Desmond asked again, directing his vile at Mark this time. When he still got no answer, he turned back to Brittney again and leaned forward. She was making a sound like she was trying to speak, but all that was coming out were sharp, kitten-like mewls. He did put a hand on her knee this time, and she barely reacted to it, only the flesh over her knee tensing slightly. "It's okay," he whispered reverently.

"It really is, you know," came a new voice, far closer to him than he would have thought possible.

Desmond jumped back and looked up. There was a tall woman in a flowing red dress leaning against the opposite side of the clown statue, her bare arms glistening against its metal frame with the sort of oiled sheen that Los Angeles women did after a tan... although this woman was pale, almost paper white, her hair an almost unbelievable shade of platinum blonde. She smiled, her lips the same red as her dress, her teeth an unearthly white.

He was reminded instantly of the grass: artificial and uncanny.

"In fact," she continued, in a voice with musical tonality. She leaned forward and touched, just barely, the short hair along Desmond's ear. "I think things are going to be lovely from this point on."

Her breath smelled like antiseptic and stained-wood, and when she smiled at Desmond his skin covered in gooseflesh.

Chelsea ran past Arthur Shane's office with a coating of thick sweat layered over her skin. She didn't even know how she'd made it so deep into the interior of the building, but here she was, limping along with one shoe through the dark halls of the office. Her breath was hard and forced, coming in ragged shovels that belayed every bad choice she'd put her lungs through in her youth.

She'd turned around three times since she'd started running, each time inviting her salty hair into her eyes and getting it trapped there. The first time he had been behind her by only ten feet, close enough that she could see from the evenness of his chest's movements that he was not having the same issue keeping pace as she was. The second time he had been closer. She didn't know how close because she had turned back around and screamed and closed her eyes and poured on the speed, her legs moving like pistons and aching immediately from it. The third time he had been farther back again, and did not seem to be quickening his pace. He followed at the super-natural pace of horror movie villains: never speeding yet always catching up.

She turned around now and found the hallway empty; at least, the parts in light.

She slowed, waiting for the man to appear in one of the beams that stretched on around the corner, wishing that she had the ability to turn the lights on to their fullest. When he didn't appear, she gasped, taking in her first full breath in what seemed like a lifetime, and looked around.

There was a maintenance closet next to her, hidden almost completely from view because it wasn't in one of the beams of light coming down from the heavens.

She turned back to the hall she'd come from again for any sign of him. If he was there, she couldn't see him.

An instant later the ache ratcheting up from her legs into her ribs made her decision for her. She pulled at the doorknob and found it unlocked, thrust herself inside, and closed the door behind her.

The light in the closet came on instantly, so bright that it stung at her un-dilated eyes and blinded her.

The closet was full of plastic do-it-yourself assembly shelves, the sort with arms made from pipes that could be snapped together into joints into any configuration one wished. The shelves covered three walls: two with individually wrapped rolls of toilet paper, and the third stacked from floor to ceiling with Crest Mint Whitening toothpaste. It was the supply closet for Arthur Shane's private bathroom, she realized.

She closed the door behind her with as little sound as she could, then fumbled along the wall to the right of it until she found the override for the lights and plunged herself back into complete darkness, her pupils having shrunk to the size of needle points while they were on.

She sat carefully, finally taking off her second shoe so that she was on even footing, her back to the largest of the three shelves, her front facing the door. As her eyes adjusted, she saw the soft sliver of dim light that was making its way into the room from under the closet's door: almost imperceptible if not for the deep black that the rest of the room was in.

She allowed herself several deep breaths, covering her mouth with both hands as she made them to muffle the sound.

A gap appeared in the light under the door, the darkness of a shadow obscuring its path. Chelsea fought the urge to make a sound as she watched it, her eyes bulging and unblinking as this void continued to move slowly across her field of view.

For reasons she couldn't quite understand, she found herself thinking of her ex-boyfriend, Gary. He hadn't been especially bad or especially good to her; in fact, until this moment she wouldn't have called him particularly memorable in any way. He hadn't even been her most recent boyfriend; she'd dated three men in the year since they'd ended their relationship, one of whom had been quite serious. She didn't know why her brain called forth the image of Gary's mustachioed face at that moment, but in its adrenaline-fuelled stupor, it did.

The shadow stopped moving across the light coming in through the edge of the doorway... then moved back until it was centered in her view, bisecting the light coming in from under the door perfectly.

It stayed there for a full minute without moving, to the point that Chelsea began to wonder if it was some trick of the way the light from the ceiling converged: the two beams not quite meeting, creating a void space in the center of the doorframe.

Slowly a second, thin shadow descended into view, erasing that wishful thought.

The door opened, and Chelsea Robbins let out a long, shrill scream.

CHAPTER TEN

There was an all-day breakfast place on Squire Street called Kevin's Bacon, the sort of family friendly place that had the menu plastered on the walls with all sorts of googly-eyed cartoon characters.

Kevin's Bacon actually exclusively served breakfast, but unlike most places that exclusively served breakfast they were open past the hours of 11-3. Kevin's Bacon was 24-7 with a sun desk out back that faced east and was high enough off the ground floor to take advantage of that fact. Between sunrise and noon, the sun bathed the deck, saturating those sitting there in vitamin D as they drank whey powder infused fruit smoothies and ate pancakes stacked so high that no reasonable diet could sustain them. They sipped coffee in the perpetually warm Los Angeles sun, and when they got too hot they ordered iced coffee and sipped on that.

The balcony was, by far, the most popular spot for writers in this side of the city. The owner fancied himself a playwright – hence the name – and spent long hours sitting in the morning sun with his laptop open to a blank page with a blinking curser. As such he was the last to shoo any other playwright or novelist out when they appeared to be on the cusp of their next masterpiece, regardless of if they had surpassed their three-refill limit or not. Famously, there was one who'd gotten a script green-lit by the House of Mouse that never bought anything at all, electing to instead bring his own strawberry water in a large clear jug from home.

Xander and Crowley sat at a table on the far left side, away from anyone else. There was a pot of deep black coffee between them that was half full, and two empty glasses of orange juice.

In front of Crowley was a large stack of waffles, adorned with whipped cream and strawberries. She had covered it in a massive amount of pure maple syrup, draining half the bottle as she had lifted each waffle with her fork to make sure she got between each layer, and not merely over the top.

Xander had an item from the menu called Kevin's Feast, which had been three pieces each of ham, eggs, sausage, bacon, and toast, as well as a small stack of waffles. Every dish at Kevin's came with waffles. There were no gluten free options at Kevin's, as every available surface had, at one time or another, been spattered with waffle batter contaminants. So far he had only eaten a piece each of the meats and a single bite of one of the waffles to confirm that it was, in fact, filled with buttery goodness.

"I don't know how you can do that," Crowley said, just before she pushed a forkful of waffle and whipped cream past her teeth.

"What?" Xander smiled. He looked around for his superfluous misdeed.

She swallowed, covering her mouth with one small hand when she spoke again, not wanting to show him the cream that was no doubt forming stalactites between the roof and floor of her mouth as she chewed. "Eat the waffles dry like that."

He held his hands apart as if to give view to the scene of the crime that was his plate.

She laughed at him. He went back to eating his bacon, which he did without the use of a fork and knife, picking up each rigid, crispy strip and taking bites out of it as though it were jerky. After a moment, their interaction faded and she saw him retreat into thought, which he'd already done three times since they sat down, each time prompting her to come up with something funny to draw his attention back.

She watched him watch people. He didn't watch people the way normal people did. Normal people took notice when someone entered a room, or walked by them, or did something odd that got them noticed… Xander *watched* people. She saw the way his eyes fell over people when they came onto the balcony, sizing each one of them up as though he were checking off stats for each of them. She watched him and wondered what he thought about each person as they came in – was he measuring their height and weight? Could he tell somehow by the way their coats bunched if they were carrying a weapon, like all the super-smart detectives in the shows she used to watch? Did he assign each person a number based on how dangerous he judged them to be, and if the number got too high, would he know something was wrong?

He watched them without watching them; he watched who they were, but also how they moved, where they went in the space. She was convinced that, even though his back was turned to half the balcony, he knew where each and every other diner was. His eyes moved over them as he ate the last of his bacon, moving from one to the other as if on a timer.

"What did you do before… this?" she asked. The words were out of her mouth before she'd taken time to consider them, and unlike her last three attempts at conversation, they weren't jovial. Her tone had the breathiness of a sigh without being melancholy, full of a sort of resigned truth.

His attention snapped back to her. "What do you mean by… this?"

"I don't know what to call what you do. It's not private investigation, it's not police work… what would you call it?"

He folded his fingers in front of the lower half of his face. Although he tried to maintain eye contact with her, they darted quickly – imperceptivity – when a lone man who had been sitting at another table stood up abruptly. "Hunting," he said after a protracted delay, so much so that she had thought he might have ignored her question. He watched the lone man walk back into the main restaurant until he was gone.

"Okay," she said. She was smirking and had one eyebrow raised. "What did you do before you hunted?"

His mouth twitched as though he were thinking of something that made him uncomfortable.

"I'm sorry," she said.

"No, it's not… no. It's fine, I just can't… really think of a time before this."

A long silence passed between them. She maintained her gaze at him and he avoided eye contact, looking down at his food.

"I mean, I used to code a lot. I used to like technology… I still do, but it's hard to keep up with it. It moves so fast now, and if it's not your life, you get left behind. I used to like playing pool, that was always fun. There was this arcade that had old coin-operated machines – kinds you really don't see anymore. It wasn't much, really, it was just killing time, but it was how I unwound. With friends."

She snorted.

"What?" he smiled.

"Nothing, it's just… I can't picture *you* just, you know, heading down to an arcade to play video games or watch Star Wars or something."

"I *love* watching Star Wars."

She pointed at him with her whole palm as she took another bite of her waffle. "See, yes, me too! But I can picture me doing it, but it's hard to picture you doing anything except… what you do. You know, the stuff with --"

"Fields," he said, finishing her thought with a name she wouldn't have said.

The noun sat between them on the table, like a golem.

"Why are you so fixated on him?" she asked finally, her brow furrowed. He looked as though he were going to respond and she stopped him: "I mean, I get it. He's bad news… you told me about some of the things he's done, even before what he did to poor Tim, but… there's lots of guys like that out there. The world is just full of nasty men, believe me."

"I know."

"So… why this one? Why not the guy stealing money from his job, or the girls being hurt by their boyfriends, or… I mean, literally anything. Anything, everything. But it's just this one guy with you, most of the time."

His face twitched again. He reached out and picked up the half-used maple syrup from the middle of the table.

"I get that he hurt someone you knew, but it's more than that now. I feel like you're over that, and that it's something… different."

Xander nodded, opened the spigot at the top of the syrup jug, then held it out to her. "He's like maple syrup," he said finally.

She stared at him, brow furrowed and mouth clenched shut for a moment. She opened it twice and closed it again, as if thinking she got it and then questioning herself, before finally responding. "Nope, don't get it. What?"

"You asked how I can eat my waffles dry," he said matter-of-factly, breaking eye contact with her only long enough to regard the jug.

"Yeah?"

He poured the syrup over his waffles. They'd gotten cold and hard so it didn't soak in the way it would have when they'd been freshly produced, instead filling every square as though they were the hastily constructed storm-breaks and it was an oncoming tidal force, barreling through each one and spilling out onto the plate. It pooled there, spreading out and growing in circumference more and more, until the eggs, sausage, and ham remaining on

his plate were all sitting in a shallow pool of maple fla-
vored corn syrup.

He put the jug down. It was empty.

"When you put maple syrup on your waffles, you
aren't just putting it on your waffles," he said, his voice
somehow both gruff and animated. He swirled his hands
over his plate as if performing some magic trick with it.
"It starts with the waffles, but it spreads out. It gets into
everything, and before you know it everything on your
plate tastes like maple. Everything's... tainted."

She winced as he bisected a sausage with his fork, im-
paled it, then held it up. The maple syrup dripped from it
and he put it in his mouth.

"That's the difference with Fields... what makes him
different. The world is full of bad men and they all need
to be stopped, but he's different. The things he does, they
spread. They get into everything. The pain he causes... it
taints everything around it."

She nodded, even as he picked up the other half of
the sausage, swirled it in some of the maple syrup, and
plopped it between his lips.

"I've been seeing someone," she said finally.

He stopped chewing. "Boyfriend?"

"Therapist."

"Oh," he paused. He looked as though he wanted to
press, then decided not to. "Okay."

"Just... trying to sort some stuff out."

"Sounds smart. I saw one for a while."

That took her aback. "I... never would have thought
that."

"You don't think I'd need therapy?"

"Oh no, you absolutely do. Like, one-hundred and ten percent, you do. I just never would have thought you'd have gone."

He smirked. "Well, if it helps your world view, I fought it every step of the way."

She snorted again. They both ate some more. "How did it go?"

"Hm?"

"The therapy."

"Oh, awfully," he chuckled, wiping his mouth with his napkin. He made several sidelong glances across the balcony as he did. "You have to want it to work, and I didn't. I wasn't in the right headspace... and the guy was an evil lunatic."

She laughed. "Do you think you'd go again?"

Xander swallowed, moving his mouth back and forth. "Maybe? I don't know. I see value in it. If you think it'll help you, do it. It's good," he said, waving his hand at her. "I just don't... there's other people out there who need that more. I'm... other people need that more."

She winced, her eyes narrowing sympathetically. "She – the therapist – she's been trying to get me to connect more," she fibbed. "And it's just... hard. I don't know how to figure out what I have in common with people, and I can't picture you doing anything to try to start, except --"

"Except pinning maps on a wall and drinking too much coffee," he finished, nodding as he poured himself more coffee.

She searched for a better way to phrase it, then nodded.

The man who Xander had watched leave returned, sitting back down at the chair opposite from the one he'd eaten at. He opened a laptop on the blank place at the table and started to type as Xander and Crowley continued to eat their breakfasts. Crowley tried to get as many different items as so could onto each forkful, while Xander ate his meats one at a time, always swallowing one before moving on to the next.

"What do you think he's writing?" Crowley asked finally, nodding to the man at his laptop.

Xander had not needed to turn to look at who she was talking about. "A fictionalized account of how his last girlfriend broke up with him, as a crime novel," he said, frankly.

"What makes you say that?"

He shrugged. "Just funning."

She snorted.

"He's single though... I can smell it on him from here."

She raised an eyebrow at him quizzically. She reached across and hovered a hand over one of his remaining ham slices, and when he nodded, took one and bit into it.

"There's no fruit smells on him, only musk and soap and those weird, artificial scents from men's shampoos. And no conditioner; there's never been any of that anywhere near his head. That doesn't just mean he doesn't use his wife's shampoo, it means he's never anywhere near them, because those floral scents are *potent*. They get into everywhere, every nook and cranny and crevice. But also: look at his plate."

Crowley turned her attention to the vacated side of the table, where his plate still sat uncollected by the restaurant wait staff.

"Half the hash browns were missed and there's ketch-up and maple syrup over the edge of the plate and onto the table from where he slipped with his knife and fork. He spilled his coffee three times while taking sips from it; twice he got the table and once he got his shirt." There was a long, teardrop-shaped brown stain on the man's shirt. "The man's a slob; he doesn't pay attention. No way does he not grab blindly and get his wife's shampoo bottle in the shower."

Crowley smirked."What if he's gay?"

"Different scents, same diagnosis."

She bobbed her head back and forth, examining the man sitting at his laptop and, from the spots of scruff missed behind his ears and the faded skin on his left hand where a wedding band had been, determined that Xander had likely been right, on all points.

When she turned back to Xander, he was tweaking the end of his own nose, then cut a triangular slice out of his waffle and ate it.

They both ate for a few minutes, and as they did she went back to watching the way he watched people, but now noticing the slight scrunches and twitches of his nose with each glance, and the way his head tilted in the direc-tion of loud sounds.

"The smelling thing… is that just, like, something you do…" she trailed off, meandering her way through the question. "Or is that, like, part of what makes you differ-ent?"

He met her gaze again and took a moment to answer. "It's a part of The Womb, if that's what you're asking. It's a part of what they did to me that I can always access… I don't even think about it anymore, to be honest."

"Does it… hurt?"

"Smelling well?"

"No…" Her mouth became something small in her face, and she started wringing her napkin through her fingers. "When you change, does that hurt?"

He clacked his tongue against the roof of his mouth. "Like you wouldn't even believe," he said after a moment, his voice almost a whisper. "It's like having your skin taken off. It's worse than that, actually. It's like having it taken off and stapled back on backwards."

She winced.

"It's never not scary. I think… I think the fear is a part of it, some adrenal reaction. I don't know, and there's nobody to ask. But I know that part of the pain is that it's *fighting* itself. The part of it that bursts out and rips through you is fighting against the part that wants to heal you, the same nerve ending screaming twice: once when it's sliced, then again when it's healed."

She nodded knowingly, although she had no frame of reference. "I noticed…" she started, then stopped.

"Go ahead," he encouraged, but in a low tone. "I can't promise I have the answers, but ask whatever you want."

Her mouth warbled. "When you're…"

"The Womb."

"When you're The Womb, you're smooth. It removes definition, except muscle definition. There's no… no appendages. No male appendages."

He sat up, just a little. "I'm not sure it is male. I'm not sure it's gendered."

She squinted, nodding. "Does that hurt too?"

He paused long enough that she wasn't sure he was going to answer, then started to nod, stopped, and shook his head. "Yes and no," he said finally. "It starts to, but the brain has a gating mechanism for pain. I think it overrides it pretty early into the process."

She nodded. "Sorry."

"It's alright."

The waiter came and took their dessert order.

Xander and Crowley stepped into the kitchen of their apartment trough their entrance, then they both came up solid against an invisible wall as they noticed Lisa.

She was standing in the living room, far enough back away from the map that they could see her, but clearly looking at it. One arm was rested on her abdomen, and the opposite hand was up at her mouth. She'd chewed each of the nails on that hand down to by half an inch as she stared wide-eyed at the map, and there was a single line of red around the nail of her thumb.

"Lisa?" Xander asked, stepping forward, the trace of a smile that had been on his face as he'd entered disappearing.

She turned to him. Her eyes were wet but she hadn't cried, and he only now noticed that the hand resting at her middle also clutched two green pins.

"There's been another one," she said, clearing her throat.

He sighed.

"It's different than before."

CHAPTER ELEVEN

Duncan opened the door to Tim White's home without trying the buzzer this time, gratefully finding it unlocked. He paused for a moment as the door shut behind him harder than he would have liked, considered taking off his shoes, then left them on and stepped into the house proper.

Tim was in the same place he had been the last time he'd been there, his headboard against the nearest wall and the rest of him centered in his living room.

He could see even in profile that Tim had an annoyed look on his face, even as the light on the camera that faced the door turned green.

"I'm sorry." Duncan said, stepping into the room with a huff and a forceful stride. He was holding a single piece of paper clutched and bent between his thumb and finger, waving it like a white flag. "I know you don't want anything to do with me, I get that. That's a club with a waiting list to join, if you want to know you aren't alone... but this coast ain't mine and I cannot get my head around this, White. I woke up to a broadcast about another one last night, and I'm telling you, I can't --"

"Chelsea Robbins," Tim interrupted in an even, measured tone.

Duncan stopped in his tracks three feet from the bed, the name jolting him as though he'd just met an invisible brick wall. "Pardon?"

"The victim. Chelsea Robbins, thirty-two, single. Worked in statistics and data management for Shane, and early this morning was found by a janitor in a fourth floor maintenance closet – that is what you're holding, I assume?"

Duncan lowered his piece of paper and squinted, turning his head.

A look of unease passed over Tim's face. "There wasn't another one... was there?"

"... No," Duncan replied, stepping forward the final few paces until he was fully next to Tim's bed. He could see the screen now: the picture of Chelsea that had appeared on her Shane employee ID card large on the let-hand side of his screen while a second window full of text covered the rest of it. It was the same photo and text on the crumpled sheet of paper he clasped in his hand, albeit much larger and crisper. "Are you... helping me?"

Tim's mouth twitched into a frown, and he made eye contact with Duncan for the first time since he'd entered. "It would appear so, wouldn't it?"

Duncan shifted from foot to foot uncomfortably. He stopped, looked down at the sheet he'd printed, then lay it down on the table that hovered above Tim's waist. "Why?"

He made a low sigh that was more like a growl.

"Because as much as I abhor the way you do your business--"

"Oh, fuck off," Duncan started, his voice high with consternation.

"—that doesn't do anything to stop the fact that there's someone out there, killing people... and if you're going to fuck this up, I'd like it to be *in spite* of the fact that I helped you, not *because* I didn't." He had finished without skipping a beat during Duncan's protestation.

Duncan took a deep breath through flared nostrils, swallowed, then nodded. "I do need help," he said.

Tim clicked his mouse twice with sweeping, left-leaning clicks. A new image of Chelsea Robbins cascaded to the front of the windows displayed, one infinitely less photogenic than the washed-out employee ID photo had been.

In it she was sitting, slouched against the tubing shelf of the janitor's closet. There was a long gash across her neck that was deep red with white freckles in its center, Tim's glorious high-definition screen picking up every intimate detail of the wound.

The toilet tissue on the shelf behind her had been dyed a deep crimson with her blood.

"Jesus," Duncan said in a hushed tone, his cheeks going pale.

Tim's front door opened again.

"Tim, there's been another one," came an urgent male voice, before the door was even closed.

"It's different than before," interjected a feminine voice.

"I'm telling him. It's different than --" Xander stopped

so suddenly that Lisa, who had been just a pace behind him, was brought up into his shoulder. He stopped as though he'd come into contact with a wall, the way Duncan had just a moment before. "Oh… I'm sorry."

Duncan's brow furrowed. "No, it's me. I didn't think he'd have an appointment." He picked up the papers he'd placed on Tim's floating desk and placed them into the crook of his arm as if they were well-organized and not a crumpled mess.

Xander turned to Tim, immediately frustrated that the man wasn't able to return his gaze. Lack of eye contact made the sort of situation-deduction that circumstances like this required close to impossible.

Duncan extended an arm. "Duncan Taggart, FBI."

Hesitating only slightly, Xander took it. "Michael Kennessy, District T--"

Tim coughed, suddenly and loudly.

"—en," Xander finished, barely missing a beat and maintaining eye contact. "I'm with PD Ten."

Lisa looked from one to the other as they shook, the fingers on her hands intertwined nervously. She walked past them as they disengaged and went to Tim's bedside. "Did you get any different information than they have on the news?" she asked. She touched his arm as she sat down next to him, the tenderness of the motion detached completely from the tension of the situation.

"I'm sorry, I'm not sure what you mean. I've been working on researching the murders at Shane," Tim said.

Xander broke eye contact with Duncan, having been still attempting to get his measure of the man. "Pardon?" he asked, forgetting himself.

"That's on me, like I said," Duncan said to the back of Xander's head.

Xander stepped forward into Tim's available eyeline, even as he was minimizing the picture of Chelsea Robbins on the screen. "Two kids went missing last night," he said matter-of-factly.

"Two is weird," Tim said, bobbing his eyebrows.

"That's not what's weird," Lisa said, pointing to the article on the Sommerfield Center as it came into view on Tim's feed. The headline that came up made the issue Lisa was talking about clear: "Body found at Sommerfield Kidnapping Site." The photo was of the long, narrow alley that existed between Sommerfield and the pastry shop next door.

Tim swallowed. "One of the children was murdered?"

"No, it was a dump. Someone went to Sommerfield and dropped off a dead body, then went inside and took two more kids."

Tim looked from Xander, to Lisa, and then finally to Duncan.

"Don't look at me," Duncan snapped, motioning toward Tim's screen with his paper. "Call it up."

Tim moved the window with the news report to one side, then tabbed open the federal RRS feed he was updated from and refreshed it. In a blink, the list of stories that had been on it were pushed further down the screen, replaced by the newest files opened in the past few hours.

"There," Lisa said, pointing at the file on Sommerfield again. She smudged the screen with her fingertip when she did, and although it bothered Tim, he said nothing to her about it. She also touched his shoulder as she got his attention in a daughterly way that more than made up for a bit of oil on his monitor.

The file opened, and along with the picture of the alley that had been provided by police to the media, there was a photograph of the dead body. It was a young adult male with acne scars dotting the edges of his hair line and a noticeable herpes sore on his pale lip, along with a straight red line through the left side of his neck, stretching from his collarbone to nearly the base of his chin.

Lisa turned white and looked away from the screen.

"That's --" Tim started.

"Not one of the missing kids," Xander finished, his voice gravelly and dour.

CHAPTER TWELVE

Crowley sat on the countertop of Xander's kitchen, her legs dangling over the side where they kept their cereal, hanging loosely in the way they did just before a doctor was about to test your reflexes. The heels of both her palms were pressed flat against the chipped edges of the countertop, her fingers curling back over their lip as she angled her body forward until it was at a forty-five degree slant with her upper thighs.

She still thought of it as *Xander's* kitchen and not her own, she realized as she leaned her head back, feeling the muscles in her neck go taut as the stretch revealed the nape of her neck. Parts of the apartment were hers – her room, her bed, her cupboard – but the communal rooms she still had yet to process as shared space: they were Xander's rooms, and she was merely occupying them.

On the countertop next to her was an open Styrofoam container with two waffles, one sausage, and one slice of ham in it, the doggie-bag leftovers from their breakfast at Kevin's Bacon.

She took out the sausage and took a bite, then closed

her eyes and leaned forward into her stretch again, alone in a place that wasn't hers.

Brian Kissliack had been a second-generation Russian immigrant, born and raised in Compton Los Angeles until the age of seven. His parents had immigrated with his maternal aunt after she'd come out of the closet first as a lesbian and then as progressive, both of which were enough to cause political strife in their community. When his aunt Constance had made the choice to flee to America, his newly married parents had chosen to come with her to support her in starting a new life in the Land of Opportunity. Brian had been born less than a year later, and three years after that they began a small deli. They hadn't been aware of the reputation of Compton when they had immigrated: they had heard the name, and in Russia, all famous American place names were held in equal parts awe and disdain, with none gaining favor over any other. The deli had to be opened away from their home to avoid insurance issues.

After four years of running the business successfully, all four had decided to take a trip home to Russia, a glorious three week event to celebrate their parents – Brian's grandparents' – fortieth wedding anniversary. It was on the trip back that had caused trouble, but ironically enough, not from the Russian side of the equation. When coming back through LAX airport they had been stopped at customs, and that was when Brian had learned, for the first time, that his parents and aunt had not legally immigrated to the United States. They were denied re-entry into the country, but Brian – a U.S-born 'dreamer' -- could not be denied entry. While his parents and aunt worked to sort out their situation, Brian had been placed in the Sommerfield long-term care facility to be looked after by the state.

He had only been there three months when he had gone missing in the middle of the night, without packing a bag or taking any of the meager belongings they had brought from his home in Compton.

That had been eleven years ago.

Brian's photo, now fully eighteen years of age although he looked much older, his face pockmarked with acne scars and sores and deep cut with an upward tilt across his neck, was still open on Tim White's computer screen. He'd been identified by his fingerprints – badly scarred though they had been – which had been taken when he'd entered the Los Angeles child care program. His body had been found in the alley outside the Sommerfield care facility, less than forty meters from where he had last been seen a decade prior.

"That doesn't make any sense," Duncan said, turning the screen towards himself without noticing that this made it much more difficult for Tim to read.

"It always makes sense," Xander said. He was outside on the balcony, squatting in a ray of sunlight and massaging the bridge of his nose between both his thumbs. A cigarette was smoldering in his hand, his third since they'd pulled up Brian's file from the FBI database. The sliding glass door to the balcony was open so that he could still speak to Tim, nobody minding that he was breaking the house's traditional rule about allowing cigarette smoke a path back into the house. "We're just too dumb to see how it makes sense."

Duncan looked up from the screen and across Tim to object to that, then he saw the scowl on Xander's face and realized that the assertion was mostly self-inflicting.

Lisa was sitting on the couch on the opposite side of the room, leaning hand and arms over the back to watch Duncan and Tim as they read the file. She'd started to tear up during their account of Brian's disappearance, but had managed to steel herself and had stayed out of their eye-line while she had.

Xander took a deep drag of his cigarette, feeling the heat from it as the ember got closer and closer to his fingers, staining them in brown and yellow rings. He could hear the crisp, crackling sound of the dry paper burning, so much like leaves on the bonfires he'd enjoyed in his youth. By the end of the drag the cigarette was at its filter, and he crushed it in the same black smudge on the balcony as he had the previous two. He picked up all three butts and brought them to the can near the balcony's edge, where he'd stood with Crowley a few days before.

He sat with his palms on the ledge of the balcony and looked over the horizon at the city.

"Is it possible it's not related to the kidnappings?" Duncan asked, looking over the notes Tim had made. There was a grainy photo of the map Xander had pinned to his living room wall amongst them, taken with an aged cell phone camera. He glanced at the green pins, then continued scrolling down. "There's a lot here. Crossover happens... you do this long enough, you realize crossover happens."

Lisa cocked an eyebrow at him, her lip curled. "That's too coincidental."

"Coincidences happen."

"If your mom is dead and your dad is standing over her with a butcher knife, is that a coincidence?"

He frowned. "I'm saying sometimes it is. Sometimes your mom had a heart attack and your dad rushed over to help without putting down the knife he was using to cut steak. Sometimes your mom trips and gets a knife caught in herself when she falls and your dad rushes over and panics and pulls it out. I'm saying coincidences happen."

"Right there," Tim said, his voice thick with consternation. "That right there is why we never worked as partners."

"*Enough*," Xander said with emphasis, turning to look over his shoulder back into the house. He thought of the entanglements that had occurred where there had been two serial killers active in his home town at the same time, as statistically impossible as that had been, and the lives that had been lost while one was in prison and the other at large, and the assumption that the terror was over. "Coincidences happen. Occam's Razor does not always err on the side of logic."

"What?" Duncan snapped, furrowing his brow.

Lisa rolled her eyes.

"This kid was missing for *ten years*. We only went back six months looking for missing kids," he continued, as though Duncan hadn't spoken.

Lisa's mouth slacked as she thought of the amount of pins on Xander's map. She hadn't realized the timeframe had been so short, and she felt a shudder work its way from her heart up to the space behind her eyes again.

"*If* Brian is linked in with the kids that went missing, then our timeline needs to stretch way farther back. Years back, like, a decade back." Xander paused, thinking of the blonde woman that had appeared in the security footage he and Lisa had found of Luka Patel being kidnapped. "And some things won't make sense, but it fits together somehow. But if Brian's disappearance and showing up dead is linked in, then we should be able to trace the pattern back further."

"What pattern?" Tim huffed, saying the words as though they were a curse. He scrolled back up to the grainy image of the map they'd passed with several deft swipes of his fingers. When the map was back on the screen he continued, "This isn't a pattern. This is just every kidnapping that kind of seems like it maybe sort of is a little like the Patel kid, but there are only so many ways you can snatch a child."

"You'd be shocked."

"Would I?"

Xander slammed his fist down against the wooden rail of the balcony, splitting the skin on his knuckle.

Lisa jumped.

Tim frowned.

"… Look," Duncan started, placing both palms in front of him in a calming motion. He took a breath, then turned and motioned to Xander. "I understand your impulse, I really do. But if you open your search up to include every kid that's gone missing in Los Angeles for the last ten years, you will drown in the research. That is too much to go through, too many files, too many *miss*-files, too many everything. That is thousands of man hours. You will be old and gray before you even find the pattern, let alone any of the kids."

Xander cursed, then turned back toward the cityscape and lit his fourth cigarette since stepping outside.

Lisa clicked her tongue against the back of her teeth, her brow lowering and creasing in the middle as it always did when she was deep in thought. She got up slowly, first kneeling on the couch and rising like a meercat whose attention has been perked, then standing alongside the couch, then finally walking out from behind it with slow, distracted steps.

Tim's eyes turned to her as she came into view, the knuckle of her right index finger resting between her teeth as she thought. "Lisa?"

Her gaze shifted to him, but otherwise she didn't move.

Xander turned back over his shoulder and Duncan turned his attention to the blonde woman.

"What are you thinking?" Tim continued to prod.

"We…" she started, frowned, swallowed, then continued with full confidence in her voice. "We don't *need* to look for all the kidnappings in the last ten years. Even all the kidnappings around care facilities."

Xander turned toward the house again, leaning against the wooden edge of the balcony. He took a puff of his cigarette but did not speak, listening to Lisa without being able to see her.

"All we need to do it look back and see if there were any other kidnapped kids that were found after like, a really long time. Found dead."

Xander stood up straight. He dropped his cigarette to the floor and crushed it out with his foot as he stepped back inside, immediately turning to Lisa.

She turned to him when he entered. "That's got to be a smaller net to cast… right?"

"Still, that's –" Duncan started.

Xander pointed to him to shut him up. "We can cross-reference that then, find out where they disappeared from, under what circumstances; that'll weed out the outliers." He stepped forward and took Lisa's forehead between both his hands, brought it forward, and kissed her where her forehead met her hair. "You are a motherfucking genius," he said.

Her nose curled as the smell of nicotine from his hands wafted over her, but she smiled.

Xander stepped over to the side of Tim's bed opposite Duncan and moved the screen back to its rightful position, aimed directly at Tim. Tim was already searching the FBI database for missing person's cases involving minors that had been missing for over a year.

Xander turned the screen towards him by pressing his thumb against its corner, even as Lisa turned and left the room. She walked out onto the balcony instead of toward the couch, stopping when the slight, almost imperceptible swell of her stomach rested against the wooden rail. Her hand touched the dent where Xander had struck and she traced the familiar lines of his knuckles, looked out over her city, closed her eyes, and wept silently with her back turned to the men.

On the screen was an excel spreadsheet filled with the names that Tim had downloaded, based on their search criteria, from the FBI database. It had been filled in line by line, pulling its data one positive result at a time with agonizing slowness, taking so long that she and Xander had made coffee for each of the four in Tim's kitchen, and that Duncan and Tim had begun to discuss the possible issues surrounding Chelsea Robbins and the remainder of the Shane victims.

When it finally stopped the database made a chiming noise that drew all four of them back to the screen.

There were seven hundred and sixty-two accounts of children that had gone missing from secondary-care facilities or such places only to show up dead years later, with the earliest known victim having gone missing in 1962.

"That's not possible," Xander said in a hushed tone. His pupils were darting back and forth in their sockets in a manic, unfocussed, REM-like manner that Tim had never seen before, as though some part of him were attempting to constantly re-examine the math of the situation and failing to come up with a solution that made sense to him.

The math of the situation was damning, Tim realized.

"It's an old guy," Duncan said matter-of-factly, taking the dry rolled cigarette from behind his ear. "Could be a woman, but it's never a woman when it's like this. It's a guy who started young in the sixties and has somehow never been caught."

"Never been noticed," Tim amended.

Duncan nodded. "Highest murder rate in the country, and missing for so long before being matched to a homicide that there was nothing left for investigators to do once they got the case. I mean – ten years later a body turns up? The site of the kidnapping could have been bought, renovated, and burned down by then. Witnesses will have died. Time will have happened."

Xander thought back to the footage of Luka Patel going missing in the secluded alley, of the gaunt blond boy that had waited with him, and the woman in the dress that had eventually appeared to collect them both. He shook his head. "It can't be back that far."

Tim furrowed his brow, turning his gaze to Xander. He squinted. "What haven't you told me?"

Duncan looked up.

Xander licked his lips. "I like someone for the kidnapper," he said finally, looking at the list but thinking only of the blonde woman in the red dress.

"When were you planning on telling me this?"

"I'm telling you now. It doesn't match up though, she's --"

"She?" Duncan asked, raising an eyebrow.

"She's max thirty, but if I'm being honest, I wouldn't put her a day over twenty-five," Xander finished. His eyes were still darting over the screen. "Send this to the printer?"

"Of course," Tim said. "I don't need to tell you to go back to the first few?"

"Obviously," Xander nodded, standing up straight and moving over to the printer to wait for the spreadsheet to start to appear.

"It's got to be a legacy," Duncan said, slowly rolling his cigarette between his thumb and forefinger. Tiny scraps of nicotine were falling out onto Tim's bed, beneath the notice of either man. "Like, she was kidnapped back in the day and got stockholmed, and now he's dead and she's doing the dirty work."

Xander bobbed his head from side to side, considering that.

"It doesn't matter," Lisa said, reappearing in the doorway. There was no trace that she had been crying on her face or in her voice, and neither Duncan nor Tim had any idea she had been. Xander could smell the salt. "We've got what we need to get her, however it happened; that's all that matters."

Xander nodded and took the first sheet off the printer, its ink still warm.

CHAPTER THIRTEEN

Arthur Shane threw the thick newspaper down into the center of the long, stretched-oval desk with considerable effort. It landed with a wet smack, weighted down with dampness from the humidity of the morning. The headline read 'Fourth Murder at Shane Complex.'

"What the actual fuck?" Arthur asked, motioning to the paper with all his fingers. He was standing at the head of the table with two drinks next to him: one coffee – steam tumbling out – and one wine – chilled to snowy edges. He took a gulp from his wine, then motioned to the paper with his glass again. "No, really. Somebody tell me what the fuck is happening?"

Sitting away from the table was a tall, sharply dressed twenty-something woman with thick-rimmed glasses and a purple streak in her hair, but who otherwise was dressed to impress. She was leaning against the bay window that gave the Shane boardroom its view of the city, gazing out over its skyline. "Dad," she said firmly, without turning to look at the scene playing out behind her.

Arthur's cheeks reddened slightly. He turned and regarded her. "Erica?"

She did not turn back to him, her gaze running over the ebbs and flows of the buildings that dotted her field of view.

He turned back to his board and took a drink, this time from his coffee mug.

There were eight other people around the table.

Grace Bennett was a Trinidadian native, half black and half Asian by ancestry. She had been hired after Shane had begun to receive public scrutiny for the absence of any minority groups or non-male gendered individuals on their board of directors. As such, they'd hired Grace to cover both bases. She had been the manager of a pesticide distributor that Shane had bought at an exorbitant fee just for the purpose of acquiring her. Since that time she had been subject to both the eyes and hands of her coworkers, but she had put up with it, sacrificing personal dignity and comfort in the workplace for the wealth that her position at Shane provided.

Samuel Laurence was a gaunt man with hanging bits of flab under his arms, leftover flesh from previous attempts at losing weight. He had dark black rings under his eyes, the type that made flesh begin to look uncanny and dead, a condition his stepdaughter had once called Zombie Eyelids. He'd run – but not been the public figure of – a skin care company that had worked to find innovative delivery methods. His company's stock had plummeted after a Sixty Minutes piece on the business revealed that he had let children overseas work in dangerous conditions, knowing full well that the heavy equipment they were using was not up to code. He'd sold the patents for his delivery mechanisms to Shane in exchange for a permanent seat on their board.

Walter Haybrook was a well dressed, trim old man with most of the colour still in his hair. He'd been Laurence's partner, and when twenty-three of those child laborers were killed in an explosion that their company knew could conceivably have happened, he'd used his ties to United States senators and judges to make sure that a no-fault settlement was reached. He'd joined to board with Laurence, at a lower equity split.

Daniel Harvey had been a successful manager of over a dozen childcare facilities in California that had been bought by Shane, primarily as a part of the *Shane Cares* initiative, but also because of their proximity to sites like Port Haven and Black Springs. Daniel's controlling interest had been bought at over five times its market value, and a seat on the Shane board of directors.

Peter Andrews was a legacy seat who had been on the board as long as Arthur himself. His son Grayson Downey was sitting next to him, having been bequeathed half his father's equity on his eighteenth birthday, and had sold half of that back to Shane in exchange for voting rights on the board.

Carl Silvereski had owned the patents for three of the field's emerging leaders in cancer-fighting medications, which he had agreed to a royalty-split with Shane for in exchange for a seat on the board and three-point-five million dollars.

Finally there was David Jill, a portly man with sagging earlobes who had simply bought his way into the upper-echelons of Shane's management, a feat that had cost him a half billion dollars, which he had never once yet regretted.

The eight of them looked at the paper that had landed between them for a moment, then back to Arthur.

Arthur rubbed the bridge of his nose, reached for his wine, then stopped himself and took another shockingly large gulp of his coffee. "Tyler Carter has been moving forward in San Diego with his restructure of the tactile division. I think we should move up our timeline to --"

"The stock dropped fifteen points," Haybrook interrupted, glowering at Shane from underneath hooded eyelids. "What's being done about this?"

Arthur looked at the paper, then motioned to it with a futile gesture. "There are Federal agents investigating. I'm not sure what else I can do, except cooperate."

"Have there been any disgruntled employees with access to the floors they'd need access to?" Laurence pressed, stroking the edges of his mouth in a way Arthur had never seen anyone else do.

Erica moved back from the glass and turned to walk out of the room without so much as glancing in the direction of the Board.

"There's nobody I'm aware of," Arthur swallowed, watching his daughter leave. "We have checked personnel files, but nothing jumps out. There's nothing on the security footage either; somehow it was all made to go to snow."

"That's a feat in and of itself," Bennett chimed, squinting.

"*Fifteen points!*" Haybrook interjected again with anger for emphasis.

Arthur took a seat, and a long swallow from his wine-glass.

Between McGreggor's Scottish Pub and the Fusion Laundromat was a small alley that, depending on the view from which one approached it, seemed to fade into the brick of either building and not be there at all. When one walked down the steps of the alley until they stood two floors below street level, there was an entrance to a bar that had, appropriately, been named The Brew. It was named that not only because of its fine choice in alcoholic beverages, but because trouble just seemed to brew there.

The Brew was well hidden, and didn't show up on Google Maps or Yelp or Zagat. There was no signage on the street alerting unknowing passersby to its presence. Word of mouth was nonexistent, as it wasn't talked about much by the people that went there. Those who found it wanted it to stay hidden. In the 20s the location had been a speakeasy, if the owner was to be believed, and he enjoyed maintaining that position.

As evening fell over the city, there was one new patron in The Brew who had heard about it from word-of-mouth.

Crowley opened the door and stepped inside. There were easily two dozen patrons inside the bar, all of whom had their backs to her, occupied by their own conversations or games or being hunched over the bar. A few heads turned at the sight of the open door, and one set of eyes lingered on her for longer than she would have liked.

There was an empty seat at the bar and she walked

to it with small, measured steps. When she reached it she waited until the few people who had turned to look at her stopped looking at her, then took a seat on the stool and leaned onto the bar.

After a moment the bartender came over to her. He was a short, portly man with gray hair and the sort of well-kept mustache that most men were envious of, like broom-bristles. He smiled as he made eye contact with her, the sort of smile that put most people instantly at ease, and leaned forward conspiratorially. "Name's Henry. This maybe isn't the best place for someone to drink alone," he said.

"Came highly recommended," she smiled.

"Even so, I wouldn't--"

"By Xander?"

Henry paused, stiffening slightly and stopping in mid-sentence. "What can I get for you?" he asked.

She smiled.

CHAPTER FOURTEEN

Laura's Tanning Salon on Springdale Street had first opened its doors over twenty years ago. The titular Laura had not been the owner at the time -- it had been her mother Chloe's business, named for her. Chloe had been three and a half months pregnant with Laura when she'd found her husband sleeping with his secretary – who was too young to remember the last time McDonalds changed its jingle – and had promptly filed for divorce. She'd gotten half his money in the settlement – one point five million – decided she would never be under the thumb of a man again, and had gone into business for herself. The last time she'd spoken to him, he'd told her that she'd never make it without him – that she didn't have what it took. Within a year the tanning salon she named after their daughter was the most profitable on the east end of Los Angeles. By the end of year three, she had her mortgage paid early and had four full-time employees.

In the many years since its grand opening there had been good months and bad months. They had weathered two recessions – one minor and one major – two draughts (nobody tanned during a draught), and one hurricane. At some time or another they had replaced every piece of furniture, every appliance, every tile on the floor, the paint, the walls, and at least ten floorboards; the only thing that had never changed was the glass display window that had proudly displayed 'Laura's' in cursive font for just over two decades.

The glass shattered as the trashcan Xander had thrown cascaded through it, hitting in the dead center of the lower-case letter 'r' and sending sharp shards hurtling inward.

"Jesus!" Lisa shouted, her hands up and in her hair in an instant as she looked at the void where the letters had been a moment before.

Xander was already in the window frame, kicking over a stalactite of glass with his boot to make it easier for Lisa to enter. He dropped to the floor with a solid thud, the gravity of him seeming to increase with his ire.

A wall mounted keypad near the cash register started to beep harshly. His gaze found it quickly and he marched over to it, his steps heavy with intent. It was beeping loudly, with the sort of escalating rapidity that alarms did to let the user know that, if they didn't act soon, it would proceed to alert the authorities.

Xander looked at the keypad, then down at the desk in front of him, then at the walls around them. There were no pictures, just inspirational quotes and idioms.

There was one stenciled above the broken windowsill: *"Art, freedom, and creativity will change society faster than politics."* – Victor Pinchuk.

He frowned, then pressed 3733 on the pad, each translucent green number lighting up as his finger touched it.

The alarm chirped off.

Lisa let her hands down out of her hair, holding them out before her as if displaying the scene to someone else who was watching. "What the hell was that?" she asked, her voice high in pitch.

Xander opened the drawers of the desk one by one until he found a ring of keys, then took them and closed them all with one fluid swipe of his arm. He looked up at her without raising his head and saw that she was still standing on the other side of the windowsill. "Come on," he said, without emotion. He turned and disappeared into the salon's hall.

Lisa cursed, then carefully raised a leg and stepped over the barrier. The heel of her foot landed on a large piece of glass that had retained the shape of the letter L it had displayed, the vinyl helping hold it together. It cracked under her weight, and she cursed again.

She entered the hall behind the receptionist's desk that Xander had disappeared through and looked in both directions, unsure of which way he went until she saw his shadow moving in the light from an open doorway. "Someone's still going to notice that, you know," she chided, before he was even in sight. She stood in the door-way – the heavy key ring he'd lifted still dangling from the knob – and watched as Xander bent over the cluttered desk in the office he'd unlocked, a laptop booting up in front of him. "It doesn't matter that you disarmed the alarm, people still have eyes."

"Crimes committed on Springdale Street only have a five percent solve rate," he said under his breath in a dull tone. "And most of those five percent are suspicious circumstance deaths. Nobody's going to think on it."

Lisa looked back down the hall in the direction of the main lounge, felt a shiver, then stepped fully into the office. "How'd you do it anyway?" she asked, forcing her hands away from each opposing bicep.

Xander opened a security suite not unlike the one she'd seen him use at the cafe. "What?"

"The alarm."

He turned to her, then looked around the office at the clutter of posters: quotes, epitaphs, and inspirational messages between handmade shelves packed with novels and self-help books surrounded them. "The pad only had two numbers worn heavily, the three and the seven. Can't be a birthday, you can't make any feasible dates with those two numbers. Not many names can be made from those letters... but some, and initials are possible, but there's no pictures about..." he motioned to the walls again, then went back to the security system. "But they've run this place for almost twenty years even in this part of town and there's quotes on the wall everywhere."

"So?"

He looked up at her. "Read some of them."

She squinted, her eyes moving over the assembled images. Some were posters that had been purchased, but most were printed at home on failing inkjets and stuck up with pushpins and sticky tack.

"Art, freedom, and creativity will change society faster than politics." – Victor Pinchuk.

"Instead of trying to make your life perfect, give yourself the freedom to make life an adventure, and go ever upward." – Drew Houston.

"Love does not claim possession, but gives freedom." Rabindranath Tagore.

He smiled at her, turning back to the computer. "What four --or five -- letter word can you make from the letters D E F P Q R S that you think the owners like, even if they aren't as aware of it as they think they are?"

"...Free," she said finally, the word in each quote standing out to her like neon.

"Free."

She crinkled her nose. "What would you have done if there hadn't been any environmental hints?"

He shrugged nonchalantly. "Worked quickly and gotten in a lot of shit, I assume." He called up a long list of files, displayed with black block text on a plain white background. They were dates and timestamps, and as he scrolled up Lisa leaned in and looked over his shoulder, amazed at how long the list was. He turned and looked at her, her mouth moving as she read every tenth date that scrolled past. He smiled. "Miranda Davis was taken from the Springdale Child Care Facility almost ten years ago," he said, even though she hadn't asked. "The place burned down five years back – arson – and there aren't many businesses on the street that are still in business... LA is like a liver, it reinvents itself every six years or so. This place though, this place has been standing for twenty years." He selected a file and double clicked it. The hourglass began to spin. "The security system has been the same for at least fifteen years, the compressed video files are kept and stored on an off-site server so that the owners can access them from anywhere."

Black and white, grainy security cam footage looking

out the bay window Xander had just smashed appeared on the screen, although the businesses across the street it caught were different. It started to play, and Xander pressed fast forward.

"What would you have done if that hadn't been the case?" Lisa asked.

He smiled. "The salon provided the local PD with footage at the time. The evidence was catalogued in Tim's files, but the video wasn't actually stored there... I'm not *that* lucky."

Two images moved past the window quickly, and Xander stopped then fast forward, backing up several frames. He squinted and leaned in.

Centered in the frame of the windowsill was a small girl that Xander knew, from Tim's files, was six year-old Miranda Davis. Her hair was gray on the black and white feed, but Xander knew from her file photo that in actual-ity it was a bright shade of red. The hue of gray matched that of the dress she wore, so Xander presumed that it was red as well. She had chubby cheeks that were dotted with freckles, a small button nose, and eyes that were wide with tears and fear and confusion.

Holding her hand was a tall blonde woman, whose hair came down over her shoulders in tumbling locks. There was a ribbon in it, dark gray amidst what strands that the camera could only pick up as white. The white of her hair was almost indistinguishable from the white of her shoulders, and the gray of the ribbon was the same as the dress she wore... which were both the same shade of grey-replacing-red that Miranda's hair was.

It was the blonde woman in the red dress from the

video feed of Luka Patel being kidnapped. Her face was in profile, but she was angling it toward the window of Laura's tanning salon just slightly, a grin playing its way over her thin lips as though she were a starlet smiling for the camera.

She had not aged a day between the two images.

"That's impossible," Lisa said, leaning in next to Xander to get a better angle for the glare. "She's... it's been fifteen years. It's... the same. Not close, the same."

She turned to Xander, noticing finally that the hairs on his arms were standing on edge. For a moment she thought she could hear the sound of the womb, which was like a stomach gurgling, she was so close.

He leaned back on the chair and stared at the blonde woman, then pressed play on quarter-speed and watched as she slowly made her way across the frame of vision, gripping the little girl's hand at the wrist as she did.

CHAPTER FIFTEEN

Chelsea Robbins lay nude on the metal table between Duncan and Travis, her hair splayed around her in a circle, damp from whatever traces having been washed out of it. The long gash across her neck had been cleaned of its blood and now looked like an unrealistic Halloween prop that found its way into dollar-stores every October: peel-and-stick gashes, scabs, and stitches. Those white chunks of bone in the wound were barely visible now that the skin had less colour to contrast them, but Duncan could still see them, knowing where they had been.

Travis held either side of her mouth and pried it open, with little effort. "The blade made it all the way through the bridge of the chin," he said informatively. He placed a gloved pinky finger into the mouth and rooted around like a dentist. It eventually emerged, just barely enough to see its green tint, near the apex of the wound.

Duncan stared at her. Even though she was dead less than a day, her eyes had gotten that cloudy, milky look to them, her pupils more navy blue than black. Before his first autopsy he'd assumed that that was something that only happened in Hollywood, some flourish invented by a visual medium to relay a story beat in some way besides verbally – but Chelsea, like many before him living and dead, made an idiot out of him. Though, he reasoned, they were technically within spitting distance of Hollywood. He swallowed, stifling a laugh and regurgitation at the same time.

"Hey, you with us?" Travis snapped, his gloved back coming down on the table.

The wet sound of the rubber on the metal brought him back to reality. "Sorry. Got lost. Keep going."

Travis frowned, both his eyes trained on Duncan for once and by chance. He pressed both hands against Chelsea's hip and lifted her, then propped her up with one arm while motioning with the other. He made broad, circular motions over her buttocks without touching them. They had bruised a dark red, with spots of black and crimson mixed in. "Hypostasis along the glutes and calf indicates she wasn't moved; she was killed as we found her, sitting there."

Duncan nodded.

Travis lowered Chelsea's body back to lying flat. "I read up about you, you know," he said without looking at the man, moving on to examine the gash that ran along her neck.

"Pardon?"

"Well, not me. Someone else in the department, but we know why they sent you out here when this is clearly the last place on Earth you want to be. I know, everyone knows." He swallowed, then grabbed a pair of tweezers off his utensil tray. He pried open the wound with his thumb and middle finger, then worked the tweezers in around a loose chunk of bone with his other hand and began to work it back and forth. "I don't know why they sent you here, but this is serious stuff now. This is important, so it better have your full attention –" he pulled the bone loose, dislodging a segment of gray muscle with it. The meat now hung limply from Chelsea's neck. Travis held up the vestige, which seemed to be part of her jawbone, sliced loose. " – Got it?"

Duncan nodded, but wasn't able to speak until the shard of blood and bone was out of sight.

Crowley smirked as she watched Xander help Lisa through the entrance to the apartment they shared, holding one of her hands and resting his other one on her hip to steady her. Crowley had been standing in the kitchen eating dry cereal out of a bowl with her fingers. "You two look cuddly," she said snidely, a hint of a smirk on her lips.

They both looked up at her. They'd seen her there before she'd spoken, but the comment demanded their attention again.

Lisa squinted at her, fully inside the apartment now. "Are you drunk?"

Crowley snorted and laughed, bringing one hand up to cup her nose and mouth to quell it. She raised a finger as if to buy time to object to Lisa's appraisal, then nodded and laughed again.

"Ugh," Lisa said, rolling her eyes.

Xander turned to Lisa. "Do you need me to--"

"Need you to stay the fuck clear is what I need you to do," Lisa interrupted, without malice. She stepped forward and put her hand on the cereal bowl, made eye contact with Crowley for a long moment, then took it away from her without a struggle. "Come on," she said, taking her by the hand and leading her. "Let's get you to bed."

Crowley snorted and laughed again, but obeyed.

Xander watched them go, staying where Lisa had told him to stand until the door to the bedroom they shared closed behind them. He walked over the countertop and looked at the bowl of cereal Crowley had been eating: it was Lucky Charms mixed with All Bran and Harvest Crunch. He smiled and shook his head.

After a moment the smile faded, and he reached into his jeans pocket and produced the grainy black-and-white image he'd printed of the woman with the dress that he knew was red. In it she had turned to look in through the window, and whether she knew it or not, was staring directly into the camera, and now at Xander.

CHAPTER SIXTEEN

Crowley emerged from the room she and Lisa shared roughly twelve hours after she had entered it, the hair on one side of her head a tangled brunette mess.

Xander turned to watched her as she propped herself up against the doorway and yawned, held up a "one moment" finger to him, then made her way bleary-eyed into the kitchen and turned on the coffee percolator. He smirked, then turned back to the wall.

Two minutes later Lisa appeared in the doorway, clutching the bridge of her nose so tightly it shone bright red under her pressure. She made a clacking sound with her mouth that he had come to recognize as her growing sensitivity to the taste of her own tongue: something he'd had to experience and overcome himself, long ago.

Inside him the true womb organ twitched and rumbled to life. He winced and shifted, ignoring it.

"Sleep well?" he asked, turning back away from him.

She gave the back of his head a rueful glare, then turned to Crowley, who was watching the coffee pour into its pot as if expecting it to do something different.

"She woke up three times," Lisa spat, running her nails through her hair as she stepped over to Xander.

"Get used to that," he said.

"Shut your face." She stopped as soon as the wall with the map of Los Angeles came into view, her step jarred out of rhythm. "What the actual fuck?"

Crowley came out from the kitchen without her coffee. When she came into view of the wall she stopped short as well, her eyes widening for the first time since she'd regained consciousness.

The green and yellow tacks had been removed, replaced with tacks of every colour and hue that Lisa or Crowley could think of. They peppered the typography of Los Angeles like pox, clustering in five or six locations mainly but scattering throughout as well, with barely a borough left totally untouched.

Lisa found herself counting unconsciously, then stopped herself when some part of her limbic brain sparked to life and she realized, without having counted nearly that high, that there were seven hundred and sixty-two tacks puncturing the map. "Were you up all night?" she asked with concern, turning toward Xander.

He was pressing his lips together between his fingers, massaging them without even being aware of it, his eyes darting from one point on the map to the other, lingering, then moving again. He nodded.

Crowley stepped forward to see the configuration better, focusing in on a large array of coloured tacks around Sommerfield. "What are the colours now?"

"Years," Xander and Lisa both said, almost in unison.

Crowley winced. "I've missed something."

Lisa frowned. "We found more missing children, going back far... too far. Like, to the nineteen sixties too far."

Crowley turned back to the map, perforated with pins, and felt a chill run through her. "You're telling me each one of these is a missing kid?"

"They were," Xander said, his tone dry and analytical. "They were all found dead."

Crowley stepped back from the map, then turned and walked back around to the kitchen. She took one of her mugs down from its shelf and poured herself a cup of coffee, drank it while standing there, and then refilled it again, along with two more mugs. She brought out one each for Xander and Lisa, who took it without asking if it was decaf or not this morning, then went back and got her own.

"You need sleep," Lisa urged, resting a hand on Xander's shoulder.

Crowley watched this, then shook it off.

"Your brain's tried, and you've been looking at this too long."

He shook his head.

"That wasn't a question."

He frowned. "I don't need sleep in that same way, especially not when there's a problem like this on hand." He gestured to the map in a wide, circular, encompassing motion. "No ages or ethnicities in common. No staff in common on a large scale – there can't be over such a long period of time. No relations in common except in rare cases, no... nothing in common." His jaw made a snap sound that made Lisa jump. He'd been grinding his teeth together as he'd spoke and they had finally slipped, making a wet snap. "Seven hundred kids have gone missing then showed up dead and I can't find one god damned thing the same with any of it."

Lisa squeezed his shoulder.

Crowley made note of this again, then forced herself to look away. "Maybe you're thinking about it the wrong way then," she offered, taking a sip of her coffee. "Maybe you don't look for what's the same... maybe you need to look for what's *different*."

He turned toward her, tearing his gaze away from the map. He squinted at her, then slowly looked back, his eyes shifting from one cluster to another. He clicked his tongue against the roof of his mouth. "It needs a Z-Axis," he smiled, his voice hushed and reverent.

He touched Crowley on the shoulder, then turned to get his coat.

CHAPTER SEVENTEEN

"She was always sweet... very hard worker though. I don't mean to say that you can't be both... do you have to put that in?"

Duncan rubbed his eyes with one hand until he saw spots, the other clasping a pen over his clipboard. He ran a digital recorder next to him that had the image of old magnetic strip spools on its screen, the spools turning away neverendingly.

The man –barely – that was sitting across from him wore a white button-down shirt and looked as though that were the only attire that would have ever suited him. He was skinny and tall with a wide head and big ears. He was clutching a tablet to his chest like a shield and didn't seem to notice that Duncan was pressing his fingers into his closed eyelids hard enough to turn his vision red.

"Sir?" the man asked.

"Yeah?" Duncan said, exasperated.

"Do you have to put that in?"

"Do I have to put in that you thought she was sweet? Not unless you ate her."

"Pardon?"

"Nothing, Eric."

"It's Fenton."

"Whatever."

Fenton Byers had been Duncan's tenth interview of the day. The first had been Chelsea Robbins' direct supervisor, then her manager, then he had met with the woman who sat in the cubicle next to her, and the next, and the next, until he'd spoken to everyone in her cubicle block. Now he had moved past that to people mentioned by the people from her cubicle block, and Fenton had been mentioned by three of them as being someone Chelsea had sat with at lunch several times.

It didn't matter who they were though, they all seemed to have the same answer: a nice, normal woman. She did her job, did it well, then went home. Bit of an over-worker, but she was liked and appreciated and... at that point Duncan typically droned out and found a reason to end the interview.

"Christ," he said, shutting the door of the temp office he'd been given behind Fenton. "Doesn't anyone fuck their coworkers anymore?" He walked back to his desk and pressed the intercom button. "Send in the next rube."

There was a bench outside the Family Values Wellness Center that, if one came at just the right time in the afternoon, caught the sunlight off the nearby office building and was illuminated with the warm glow of morning for a second time. Crowley found herself sitting in the center of that bench, her arms spread out along the cusp of its back until she took up the entire thing.

The pinholes pressed into her living room wall haunted her. She didn't think she would ever look at that wall the same: that she would never see the eggshell white, only the holes punctured in it, and be reminded about what they were.

Not far from where she sat was a man in his late thirties playing with his daughter, who couldn't have been more than seven. They didn't do anything to exposit that they were father and daughter – not like in the movies, where they would refer to each other as such to make sure even the least salient member of the audience got the hint – but it was clear in how they interacted, and how they looked. They had the same sharp cleft chins, the same chestnut hair, the same shape of face. She was a tiny clone of him, running circles around him and the swing set they were on at once and laughing and growing.

Crowley felt a shudder run through her.

She remembered reading once that there was nobody as genetically similar to you as your sibling, but right now she couldn't imagine anyone whose 0.1% genetic differences were more similar than that girl and her father. He was chasing a version of himself around the playground, his hands outstretched and fingers wriggling as he pretended to always be one step behind her.

She had gooseflesh even though the sun was bright on her. The smile she'd had, briefly, while watching them encircle each other like electrons around an atom, faded. She wondered internally why they were here, and the image of them started to break at the seams – if they were as happy as they seemed, why were they playing outside the

Wellness Center, waiting to go in? She imagined the girl answering the intake questionnaire she'd been given, and wondered what a child would say to most of those items.

She took her arms down from the sides of the bench and brought them to her lap, retreating.

After a moment, she stood and went into the Wellness Center lobby to wait.

She wasn't sure where she was, but it was cold and dark. She knew cold and dark like they were old friends of hers; they'd been with her since childhood.

There had been stairs and a putrid stench and more awful, winding stairs, and then a long hallway of nothing but darkness and the smell of decay, and now Brittney sat with her legs clasped close to her chin, holding herself tight for lack of anything else to hold.

Desmond had been taken away, she wasn't sure where, and she still didn't know by the time her shaking sobs ceased and she went to sleep.

CHAPTER EIGHTEEN

"It needs a Z-Axis."

Lisa pushed the edge of the map as far as it would go, tucking it under the long-dormant space heater at the end of the living room. It wrinkled and tore as she wedged it under, but she didn't take any notice, frantically smoothing out the creases it had come folded with.

There was a loud crash behind her that she did not react to, as Xander emptied a bucket of Lego blocks out onto the glossy laminate they'd put down. There was a freshly-lit candle alongside it, sending the sweet smell of vanilla into the atmosphere of the apartment.

There were five more buckets of bricks stacked in the archway between the living room and kitchen.

They'd bought a new map, a larger map, one that focused exclusively on the tight metro region they were focused on, leaving out the suburbs and the Hollywood hills where there had been few-or-no pins. The pins he had used were in a pile in the corner, swords from a war that had ended waiting to find a new use.

They'd taken the old map off the wall -- it was crumpled in a corner of Xander's room now. This new map took up the entire floor of the living room, bunching at its edges.

"Anthony Gervais, taken from Cederbrook, went missing in 1982 at the age of seven," Lisa said, pulling a random piece of paper from the pile beside her.

Xander picked up a blank sheet of paper and tacked it to the wall behind him. He wrote '1982' in sharpie near its center, then 'Yellow Three.' He fished around the pile of Lego he'd poured and found a suitable brick: canary yellow with three bumps along its upper level.

Lisa's mouth twitched and she moved to the empty space between her papers and the pile of Legos and began to organize them into colours.

He took a random pin from the discarded pile and held it over the candle flame for a moment, then forced it through the depressed part of the Lego's ridged roof until it was flush, the metal spear sticking out its bottom. He pressed the spike through the map at Cederbrook and into the floor beyond it until the Lego block appeared to stand flush without the benefit of one of those green pegged mats typically used to build one's architecture on. "Found?" he asked.

She pushed a pile of yellow bricks she'd already made towards him. "September 1993."

He stacked yellow three-prong bricks on top of the one he'd pinned to the floor until it was eleven bricks tall. Then sat back up straight and eyed his work, counting the floors in the tower he'd made again. He shifted the map under him and watched as the pin cut a small line in the map, but did not fall over.

He nodded at Lisa and she nodded back, then reached for another sheet of paper. "Ruth Hellings, age fourteen, went missing in '79."

He danced his fingers above the pile of bricks, finally selecting a four-pronged blue cube. With his sharpie, he wrote '1979 – Blue Square' on the sheet of paper an inch above 1982, then picked up another pin and held it over the candle.

Lisa began to fish three blue cubes out of the pile she'd made of the colour – Ruth had been found in 1983.

Xander and Lisa stood up when they put the last peg into their floor, and stepped back until their backs were against the wall, getting the full view of what they'd made.

Lisa fumbled for his hand without thinking about it, finding his wrist and grasping it tightly. His hair had been standing on edge, she realized, and so was her own.

They'd seen the pattern emerging as they'd placed the bricks in place – it was hard not to –but there was something about sliding that last piece of the puzzle into place that made it *real*. Until that point, as unlikely as it had been after the first hour, there was still the possibility that they would find more sheets that broke the pattern, and revealed the towers they were seeing as nothing more than the luck of the order the files were drawn in.

They'd made a cityscape of their map of Los Angeles, Lego towers of various shapes, sizes, and colours jutting up out of the floor, like a child constructing a city for their toy Godzilla to destroy.

LA Sun had the tallest tower, a green monolith sixteen bricks high that cast a shadow over the rest with the light coming in from the window. It was surrounded by a collage of lesser towers: yellow two-stories and blue five-stories, all of which surrounded the main tower like pubic hair around a great green cock.

Sommerfield had the most towers, ranging from two to seven blocks high in a tight little cluster, burbling up from the lower right of the map as though it were growing up and bursting through from the floor beneath it. It had become so crowded that they had started to double-stack unlike colours, for fear they would start to merge and confuse its architecture with Quartz Hill.

Those weren't the patterns that gave Xander pause though. It was a large cluster of bricks on the south side of the map, at a long-term children's care facility called Joucastle.

There were thirty-seven structures there, wedged into that section away from the rest in its own corner of the map. They were a variety of colours, but the vast majority of them were different sizes of red, which Lisa had chosen to represent the current decade.

None of the towers at Joucastle were more than two blocks high, with thirty of the thirty-seven being only a single block.

Xander swallowed, then slowly lowered himself into a squat and looked at it, the red little cluster like a herpes sore at the base of the map. All the other facilities towers above it, looming like bullies – yet it was the one that seemed sinister, the one that was different and out of place from the rest.

He stroked the scruff on his upper lip, ran his fingers through his hair, then turned back to his partner. "We're bringing this to Tim."

She nodded, then turned to get her coat, stepping around the towers on the map, giving them each a wide berth.

◣◤

"How did your date go?" Susan asked. She reflexively checked her notes before she did, even though she didn't have to; they'd only met recently.

Crowley shifted in her chair uncomfortably.

"That great, huh?" she said, in a tone that was somewhere between clinical and social interest.

Crowley smiled. "It was fine. It was… nice. It was friends eating and talking."

Susan made a note, then pushed her hair back behind her ear.

Crowley winced. "He's been busy with work. Our roommate has been helping him, actually. They've gotten into this… weird? Yeah, a weird place."

"Are you worried she'll be a rival?"

She smiled at that. "I don't think she sees him like that."

Susan pointed the tip of her pen at her. "You didn't say that *he* didn't, though."

Again, Crowley shifted. "I really have no idea what he sees anything as."

She smiled, wrote something, then turned back. "The choice is what's important though. You made that leap, you asked him instead of waiting to be asked… You can't control the outcome of any interaction with another person, but you took ownership of your own agency in it, and that's huge." She kept eye contact with Crowley for a long moment. "So, if it's okay, I'd like to try and think about some of the times you've felt that kind of option paralysis and see if we can figure out what you're feeling in those moments, and how best to combat those feelings... Would that be okay?"

Crowley winced, then nodded... although she didn't feel as though she had a choice.

"I'm telling you, it was like pulling teeth," Duncan said, his voice garbled and crackling through Tim's speakers. A video feed of his face was framed in the center of the screen, shaking every few moments as though whatever he had balanced his phone on before making the video call was unstable while in use. Tim had other windows open to either side of him, scrolling through the employee files that Shane had sent on each of the victims. "You have never met boring people until you've worked in an office."

"It couldn't have been that bad," Tim droned, reading through a long stretch of sick days that Rae Stevens had taken this time last year. He alt-tab switched to a notepad app on the other side of Duncan's feed, and made a note to check it against medical records.

Duncan grabbed the camera and brought it closer. "One of them collected *stamps,*" he said. He brought his fingers to the side of his skull and then shot them outward, pantomiming his head exploding. "Letters don't even take stamps anymore, they have little pictures printed on them. You have to request the stamps *special*."

Tim smirked.

Duncan put the phone back onto its perch, rested against the keyboard and screen of his laptop. It shook with every click and press of the keys he made.

They sat like that for nearly ten minutes, each one working independently in view of the other via video feed, before Duncan's brow began to crease.

After a moment of switching back and forth between windows over Duncan's face, Tim noticed. "What?"

Duncan paused, his lip curling slightly. Tim could see the reflection of whatever he was looking at in his eyes: not clearly enough to see over the cheap camera lens, but enough to see that it was in motion, a video instead of a file. He snarled, then made a few extended, dragging clicks.

A notice popped up in the lower right-hand corner of Tim's screen informing him that there were new files in his drop-box.

"You get that?" Duncan asked. He had retrieved his cigarette from behind his ear and was fumbling it between calloused fingers again.

"Yes," Tim said, even as he was opening the folder. There were several QuickTime videos there, and he clicked the first one. It opened to a long empty hallway shot in an office building, with vending machines along one side of the frame. "What am I looking at?"

"Security footage from the night Chelsea Robbins was killed."

"I'm not going to regret opening this, am I? If I throw up, there's nowhere for it to go until the care-worker gets here."

"You sound like you're speaking from experience."

"I *am*."

Duncan winced through clenched teeth, comically. "Relax; if it was that bad, I wouldn't have been watching it--" he paused. The light in his eyes was moving and it was clear he was watching too, at a slightly different time code.

Chelsea entered the frame from the left, made her way over to the vending machines, and started punching in her selections.

"Has it happened yet?" Duncan asked.

"She's buying food."

"Wait for it."

Chelsea fished something out of the receptacle from the bottom of the machine, eventually standing with something so small Tim couldn't pick out what it was. When she cupped one hand and shook the bottle over it though, he knew it was pills. She took two, swallowed, then took a third out of the bottle and walked to the water bottle refill station a few feet away.

"Should be soon."

As Tim watched, Chelsea's head whipped around as if startled by some loud noise. She craned her neck to peer down the empty hallway that terminated off the screen and paused for a long moment. Her back was turned to the camera, but from her body language it was clear she was calling out to something on the other end of the hall. After a few moments she started to walk towards the sound, eventually disappearing from view altogether. "Something got her attention."

Duncan nodded. "Ayuh. But try and find what on any of the other feeds at the same time code and you sure can't." He looked at something, then turned back to the camera. "Open file SN-987-4 to that timestamp and see what you get."

Tim went back to the folder.

His front door opened.

His heartrate increased for an instant, still not accustomed to not being able to turn in the direction of a new sound, then he tabbed his closed-circuit camera feed onto the screen and watched as Xander and Lisa entered his home through the front door. Lisa took off her shoes; Xander did not.

"I'm on with someone," he said, speaking up.

"What?" Duncan asked.

"Xander," Tim said dismissively, opening the file Duncan had told him to.

"Who?"

Xander shot him a wide eyed look, his palms outstretched in the universal expression of 'what the fuck.' He raised one arm high above his head and leveled his fingers, as though miming someone else's height.

Lisa raised an eyebrow to him quizzically.

"Michael," Tim corrected, clearing his throat. "Sorry, brain fart."

Duncan nodded. "Tell me when you're there."

Tim looked at Xander, who held up a phone that had an image displayed on it. He bobbed his eyebrows, then turned the timestamp on the new video to just before the timestamp on the video of Chelsea had turned her head, and pressed play.

The video opened to a blank hallway for a long moment; there was a hint of motion at the far end of the hall that may have just been a flicker on the screen, and then the entire video fell into static. Tim furrowed his brow. "What the fuck?"

"Did it go to snow crash?" Duncan asked.

Tim nodded.

"It comes back after about a minute, but at the same time it moves to SN-987-5... like it's a charge bouncing between feeds or something." He paused. "Or like someone's editing something out."

Tim nodded. "Follow it." He turned his gaze back to Xander and Lisa. "I've got to go, we'll talk soon. Follow up on this though, check to see if there are feeds like this from the others. And if you get Rae Stephens's medical records, put them in the drop box for me, will you?"

Duncan nodded, then reached toward the camera, and an instant later the video cut to black.

"You said my name," Xander said right away, holding his arms up in an exaggerated shrug again. "What the fuck?"

"Sorry."

"Why do you do that anyway?" Lisa asked, walking around to the other side of Tim. Without asking, she pressed her hand against his pillow, feeling how velutinous it was, and tisked with a shake of her head. She reached under Tim's mattress and pulled out a fresh, white pillow – the sort of high-end hypoallergenic ones that they had in the best hospital rooms.

"How many people do *you* know named Xander? Have you ever tried to go incognito with a name like that?"

She rolled her eyes, then turned to Tim and smiled warmly, holding up the pillow as if to present it as a question.

"Thank you," he sighed with gratitude.

She gently lifted his head and slid out the pillow he had been laying on for well over a day, then slid the new one under and lowered him again. She fluffed it twice, pushing down starchy bits to try and keep them out of his peripheral vision. "*Remind* her," she said, with emphasis. "You're not doing her any favors. The next time I come and you've been sitting on the same pillow for over a day she's going to have to deal with me."

He smiled up at her as she grazed his cheek with her thumb, then turned his gaze back to Xander. "What do you have?"

Xander held up the phone. On it was a picture of his living room floor, covered with the map and built high with Lego towers of various colours.

Tim squinted. "Innovative."

"Thank you."

"What's it mean?"

Xander took the phone back. "It keeps track of how much time there was between the kids going missing before they showed up dead. There's a pretty wide range of turnover timeframes throughout them all... except that one in front. Place called Joucastle; hasn't shown up on our radar so far."

Tim tabbed open a browser and started to type in the name. "J – O – U?"

Xander nodded.

Tim pulled up the federal file on the facility. It was a large building, repurposed several times since its inception in the 1920s. It had started as an estate for a new-money stock trader and eventually become a speakeasy during prohibition. In the years since it had been a boarding school, a hippie commune, a private college, and now it was a long-term care facility for children. It had had fifteen major renovations in the hundred years since its construction, and thirty minor ones to repair water damage and for asbestos abatement (and later, removal).

There was a staff of forty-five and they had a good CPS rating... not great, but good. It had had only two general managers in the last fifteen years, the last ten of which was a man named Jeremy Piper. Tim pulled up the file on Jeremy, a clean-cut thirty-two year old with blue eyes and one of the close-cropped blond hairdos that usually came out of the military. He was smiling a politician's smile in his file photo, as most were.

"Why's there a federal file on him?" Lisa asked, curling her lip.

"Nothing sinister," Tim assured. "Standard OP when a child goes missing is to put the staff on file and fingerprint. Most of them have to sign a waver now to work there, especially in the private institutions."

She nodded. "Good."

"Not that it's helped," Xander leaned forward. "He's got no record?"

"No," Tim said.

"Nobody liked him for any of the missing kids? There have been, like, at least five since he took over."

"He was liked by at least one investigator, but that

sort of thing doesn't mean anything. I've liked people before and been wrong, and Mr. Piper here had alibis for each and every missing kid and for each and every body drop."

Xander squinted, then pulled out a folded sheet of paper from his jeans pocket and started to unravel it. He folded it out and looked it over. The names on it were scrawled on it in bleeding sharpie, in letters so slanted and thick that only Xander could have read it at first glance. "Yeah so, six went missing during his tenure, so far. Scott Walsh, fifteen, found three years later. Krista Board, sixteen, found two years later. Vance Trombly, sixteen, found two years later. Rebecca Paulin, seventeen, found a year later."

Lisa stood up slowly.

"David Brock, seventeen, found a year later, and Jessica Verhoven, seventeen, found just like six months later. That last one may not be one of what we're looking for."

"Tim, can you print off the excel sheet with all the kids on it?" Lisa asked suddenly and contemplatively.

Tim opened the excel file and pressed print.

"Thanks." She stepped away from the bed and floated over to the printer.

Xander shook his head. He pointed at the picture of Jeremy on the screen and tapped it twice. "He's young."

"He is."

Xander squinted. "We have anything else on him?"

Tim scrolled through the file. "Nothing probative. He was in the system himself for a few years off and on, spent his last two years being a minor at Joucastle itself actually... but there's nothing here to suggest anything."

He frowned. "Sorry. Just som--"

"We're idiots," Lisa snapped, rising to her feet. She walked back over to Tim's desk with the sheet of paper he'd printed and a ball-point pen she'd taken from next to the phone. It had the name of the company Tim's care workers worked for printed across it. She held up the paper.

"I'm sure that's not true," Tim smiled.

"No, we are. We are idiots. All this fucking around with profiling and research and graphing and Legos... and we couldn't even manage to do grade-school math."

Xander furrowed his brow and took the page. It was the excel sheet, each column a different field of data. Name, Age, Date Missing, Date Found. Lisa had scrawled the rough number of years between the Missing and Found dates between each, and to the right of each row had done basic addition.

Scott Walsh, 15, missing for 3 years. $15 + 3 = 18$.

Vance Trombly, 16, missing for 2 years. $16 + 2 = 18$.

Rebecca Paulin, 17, missing for 1 year. $17 + 1 = 18$.

David Brock, 17, missing for 1 year. $17 + 1 = 18$.

Jessica Verhoven, 17, missing less than 1 year. $17 + 1 = 18$.

This list continued past those that had gone missing from Joucastle. Rodney Baker, 7, missing 11 years. $7 + 11 = 18$. Danielle Fergeson, 5, missing 13 years. $5 + 13 = 18$.

"Motherfucker, we are idiots," Xander said under his breath. "They're all kept until they're eighteen."

CHAPTER NINETEEN

The Joucastle was a tall building on the southern edge that bordered urban and suburban Los Angeles, the strange staccato line that divided the skyscrapers from the backyards and patios. It had had land once – lots of land – but now there were mere feet separating it from the tenement building next door: a rocky path divided them, the grass having been ripped up after many long droughts.

Even when it had had land, Joucastle had decided to build *up* and not *out*. The main building was a large long rectangle of two above-ground floors. The cube reached back from the street for several hundred feet, stretching its way back towards Hollywood as if drawn to a forgotten lover. However, each of the four corners had new floors springing up, the way spires sprung up from the corners of old castles. They came up in rectangles though, not in spheres, some bizarre fusion of medieval and modern architecture.

Xander sat against the stone stairway leading up to the Frederick Douglass Memorial tenement building with both his knees huddled up close to his chest. The sun had gone, but the pavement still held its warmth, and there was a breeze on the air that carried it to him in intermittent sweeps, displacing the hair on his forehead.

He had been watching Joucastle for over an hour, had been ever since he'd gotten Lisa in a taxi home and had gotten his own going south. In that time, five people had entered and three had left: teens mostly, but a few adults, one of whom lingered outside for several minutes before leaving, looking back over his shoulder several times.

Jeremy Piper stepped out onto the front stoop of Joucastle's main entrance, buzzing a card on an electronic reader as he did. He stood at the edge of the stairway up to his building and took a deep breath, inhaling the thick night air of Los Angeles.

He was shorter than Xander had expected – shorter than him. He looked like he would have come up to about Xander's chin. He was smiling the same smile he had been in the picture Tim had had on his computer: normal and inviting. He was wearing a striped button-down shirt and a pair of tight-fitting black jeans, with a shiny belt-buckle in the shape of California on it. Xander didn't realize they made those in the shape of states that weren't Texas.

Xander watched him as he stood like a man admiring a sunset even though he was facing a Laundromat. He pulled his bangs back down over his eyes.

Crowley stood with her belly against the kitchen counter, waiting for her mint tea to cool. She had a lamp on, but other than that the only light was the ambient neon from the street which filtered its way in through the window behind her. It was cooler without the lights on.

On the counter in front of her was a half eaten piece of toast with butter and jam on it, and a stack of papers with crumbs on them. Susan had given them to her before she'd left for the day. There were three sheets in total she'd been asked to read – there had been seven in total, but Susan hadn't handed them all over. She'd been prepared for their conversation to go a few different ways, Crowley guessed.

The first one was "Doing, Being, and Mindfulness." Susan had spoken a lot about mindfulness during their session today. It sounded like meditation to Crowley, but with your eyes open, or Progressive Muscle Relaxation, without the same desired effect. It just seemed like a lot of effort – quieting your mind that much. She couldn't recall the last time her mind had been as quiet as she made it out to be.

The second sheet, "Attitudes and Commitment," was a stapled photocopy of a chapter of a book called *The Practice of Mindfulness*, which Crowley was sure had been photocopied illegally.

The third sheet was called *The Do's and Don'ts of Being Assertive*. It was an exhaustive list that seemed contradictory, with advice on the one side to not be passive being contradicted on the right to warn of being aggressive. It seemed like such a tight-rope walk – a balancing act – that she didn't think she'd ever be able to managing it in normal, natural conversation. By the time she had weighed the rules of something she wanted to say against each other, the topic would have moved on.

"Hey," Lisa said behind her, entering the apartment.

Crowley slid the sheets into a drawer, then picked up her toast and took a bite as she turned around. She smiled. "Hey!" She waited a moment as Lisa took off her jacket, then noticed that she was alone. "Everything okay?"

"Yeah," Lisa nodded. "He's checking out an orphanage that seems shady, might be late."

"Is that what the Mego-Blocks in the living room are about?"

Lisa smirked, then nodded.

"Tea?"

She nodded again.

"You can't just stay there, you know," a man said as he walked up the tenement stoop, stopping to aim his face at Xander. He pointed to a sign just to the right of the door he was heading toward. "There's no loitering."

Xander turned and eyed the sign, then back toward Joucastle. "Can't read."

"It says, 'No Loitering.'"

"Am I supposed to just take your word for that?"

The man balked. "Are you calling me a liar?"

"Why not? You're calling me illiterate."

The man huffed and stepped up two more stairs. "I'm going to call the police."

"You do that, I'm sure they'll send someone right over as soon as they're done with all the murders and assaults."

The man frowned deep, then went inside his building.

There were no upstairs lights on at Joucastle, nor had

there been for the last hour. The main floor lights were still on – they likely stayed on all night for staff --- but upstairs, in what Xander assumed were the dormitories, not a single light or lamp or source of illumination was adding to the light pollution of the Los Angeles street.

Of all of the windows with no lights, only one had appeared to have curtains drawn. The rest were just... black. In a building filled with teens, at ten o'clock at night. Not one was reading, or playing a game, or on social media, or talking to one of the others.

Jeremy had stood outside on the front step of Joucastle for nearly ten minutes enjoying the fresh air of the city, then had gone inside, and within minutes the lights upstairs had gone out, one by one.

Since then no one had come in or out.

Lisa took a sip of her tea, the third cup they'd poured. It was decaffeinated, but she had long since torn off the part of the tin's label that said that, and found that she could fool herself. She and Crowley were both sitting on their respective beds, their feet dangling over the edges facing each other, using their shared nightstand for their cups.

The papers Crowley had hidden in the drawer were on the bed next to her. She was reading by the glow of their lamp again, and Lisa had the sheet on the *Do's and Don'ts of Being Assertive* in front of her. "Apparently I am assertive as fuck," she said, warbling her mouth.

Crowley shot her a wry look. "Not funny." She had found it funny.

Lisa smiled, then kept reading the sheet. When she put it down, she did so gently, lying back over on Crowley's bed. "What does she think?"

"The shrink?"

Lisa nodded.

Crowley thought for a moment, then shrugged. "I'm not sure. I find her hard to read. I guess that's kind of the point. She's good, though... she's helping. I'd like to get back to work, but a lot of that is choosing what I want to do – and you know, choice."

Lisa winced. "How much have you told her?"

"Enough."

Her hand fell to her stomach, and she hugged it. "Nothing to feel bad about, you know. I've been thinking I should go before this little one finds his way out... just to make sure my head's in the right space, you know?"

Crowley nodded.

"I mean, lots of mistakes will have been made by the time he pops. Like, a domino-line of mistakes, one after the other, but I want them to stop once he comes out, you know? Like, the mistakes have to stop then, but I'll still be the same person who made them before, so what makes me think I know better now?"

"You do."

"Yeah but you have to say that," she smirked. "Some days I think I'd like an outside opinion."

Crowley smiled, then looked down at the papers and the smile slowly left her face.

Lisa leaned forward and put her hand on Crowley's knee, a gesture that was cliché and yet heartfelt at the same time. "Whatever you choose, you know I'm with you, right? Nothing's changed. We got this. *We* do."

Crowley nodded, then moved in and gave Lisa a hug, which was returned.

Xander had risen and walked over to the Joucastle complex, and now stood directly in front of it, staring into the light that came out of the main foyer into the street. It looked like a mouth, this great glowing mouth of a sleeping dragon, whose teeth were backlit by the fire in its stomach.

He watched as the building breathed. He'd never told anyone because he knew they'd think he was crazy, but buildings breathed. Buildings moved with the people in them, subtle movements; as dozens of people inside inhaled and exhaled, the building they were in shifted and contracted like a lung.

He watched for signs of life: a teen stealing a cigarette through a pried-open window. A light. The shadows of amorous affiliations that the religious right had warned would be the result of co-ed care facilities, and had largely been correct.

There was nothing.

The building was dead, without a single sound his ears could pick up inside: no plates clinking, no dishes being washed, no rustling of sheets. The light in the foyer was a draw, he realized: look here, everything's okay, like a bug finding its way to the charge of a zapper.

Xander sucked his lips until they made a snapping sound. "Motherfucker."

CHAPTER TWENTY

Duncan woke up on his couch, amidst a pile of personnel files from Shane. He cursed, softly at first, and then louder, then got up to change into fresh clothes and brew coffee.

The afternoon sun came to Joucastle with all the sordid heat that Los Angeles had to offer, as though the city were literally trying to make itself hell on earth. The stone of the building absorbed it and radiated it, until by mid-afternoon it became a radioactive husk in the dead center of Malbar Street.

The lights had come back on around six am, and had stayed that way until ten. People had started to come and go again then, and thirty minutes ago, Xander had watched as Jeremy Piper greeted a young couple with that same plastic smile he'd had on when he was outside taking in the evening air. They'd stayed inside for fifteen minutes, and come out smiling with the man's arm clasped around the woman's shoulder.

"Okay. I'm here," Lisa said as she walked up to Xander. She stopped a foot in front of where he was sitting, her hands on either of her hips.

He tore his gaze away from Joucastle reluctantly, as though watching it were somehow keeping it in check. He had moved to cross the street in the night when he'd noticed the laundromat there was open twenty-four seven. He'd started talking to the man working – Gupreet – who was the owner's son. They existed, primarily, through their proximity to Joucastle: they got the contract for the sheets, bedclothes, and garments. At some point they had started talking about immigration and Gupreet had made Xander coffee with natural honey to sweeten it. Some hours later Gupreet had offered to wash Xander's shirt, which he had accepted gratefully.

Xander held his third cup of the honey-sweetened coffee in his hands now, sipping it in conservative portions since Gupreet had gone home and his father had taken up the morning shift. He stood up straight and twisted his own neck until he felt the calcium pop, and nodded at her.

She looked at the coffee, then into the Laundromat, then across the road to Joucastle. "What's going on?"

"That place is wrong," he said, cocking his head toward it before taking a sip of his drink. "I'm not sure I would have seen it if I hadn't been looking – but I *am* looking, and it's just *wrong*."

She turned and regarded the building again, twisting her mouth sideways as she looked it over. "I don't see anything."

"It's hard to pin down. You ever get that feeling about a place, like an alley or a room, and just feel wrong about it? That's that place. I can't figure out exactly why, but something about it is not right, and we're going to find out what."

She nodded. "Okay, sounds good."

He regarded her for a moment, how easily she'd gotten on board. "We're going to go in as clients, like we're considering the place. We'll be pretending to be a couple, if that's not too repugnant."

She shrugged. "I've pretended to be a couple in an *actual* relationship, so this shouldn't be a stretch."

He laughed.

"Why me though? I'm sure Crowley would have, and she didn't show her face at the Sun."

He took a sip of his coffee and his gaze fell to her midriff and then back up to her face, like an elevator. "You're showing," he said finally, swallowing.

She raised an eyebrow.

Lisa clasped Xander's hand as they stepped through the foyer of Joucastle. It was larger on the inside than it looked on the out, with the type of high ceilings and open space that weren't used in modern architecture. In his mind Xander amended his internal schematic of the main long box of the building: the entirety of it was not two floors -- it became two floors in wings off from the foyer. The foyer itself was high enough to take up the space of two floors in and of itself, like a cathedral.

The walls were a pale yellow, which had added to the glow affect Xander had experienced on the darkened street last night while peering into its maw. From inside now he could see that the trim was a pale green, one so light it was almost white. He squinted as his eyes cast over the mouldings, their swirls and divots and panes. The work on them was intricate, and so high up that nobody but he and the people who changed the lightbulbs would ever have appreciated it. The room had a smell like antiseptic varnish, as though the floors were in a perpetual state of just having been done, and it overpowered everything else.

Standing near the desk at the end of the foyer and talking to the man that sat behind it, Jeremy Piper looked up as they approached and smiled wide from ear to ear, showing all his teeth and too much of his gumline in the process. He stood straight and stepped toward them, hand outstretched.

Lisa held his hand tighter, digging her nails into the flesh between his fingers without realizing it. He did nothing to correct or dissuade it. "I don't like this," she said under her breath, so low that only he could have heard. She didn't turn to him when she spoke, she kept her eyes trained on Jeremy as they approached each other across the massive hall. "I don't like that smile."

Xander nodded and gave her hand a gentle return squeeze before extending his other hand to Jeremy.

"Welcome!" Jeremy said, his voice practised and polite, somewhere between a customer-service voice and a radio voice. They shook hands firmly. "Did you have an appointment?"

"Yes," Xander nodded, before Lisa could speak. "The Drew family. We made an appointment to look around?"

Jeremy smiled, then turned back to the person behind the desk, who was already tracing her pen down over the side of a planner. He lifted his head, then shook it. "Drew?"

"Yes. Like Nancy Drew. Xander and Lisa Drew."

"That'd be a good name," Jeremy said, turning his attention to Lisa's stomach as if to make eye contact. "You don't see many Nancy's anymore."

"We think it's a boy," Xander corrected.

Jeremy smiled. "How nice." He turned back to the receptionist, who shook his head again. "I'm so sorry, we're not seeing you."

"Oh, I'm sorry," Xander said, his voice taking on a tone of exasperation. He reached over and laid a flat, gentle palm on Lisa's stomach. "We're just – we're considering adoption as a possibility, and we wanted to take a look around, you know? Make sure it's not like it was in the old movies."

Lisa shuddered as Xander removed his hand.

"Of course," Jeremy smiled that gummy smile again, his eyes darting to Lisa's abdomen over and over again. It was like a man trying desperately not to look at a woman's breasts while fighting the overwhelming urge to do so, like his pupils were on a swivel. He turned and smiled at the receptionist, and nodded.

Lisa closed the small gap between she and Xander, and he didn't think it was a part of their act.

"Well, I'll make some time of course," Jeremy said, holding out his hands. "It's an important decision after all."

"Yes," Xander said, nodding. "It really is."

The pale yellows and greens continued into the hallway that spawned off to the right of the foyer, and Jeremy commented on them as they went through, boasting that some of them were over fifty years old. "You can't have that in some places. In some places the children would have ripped that to shreds: we make sure a child's needs are met here at Joucastle though, and there's less delinquency as a result. Far less."

There was a pass-through in the wall of the hall that gave a brief view of the kitchen before they reached it. It had three stoves, four fridges, and a deep freeze, along with the sort on in-wall pantries that most buildings designed pre-electricity had. There was a huge amount of cutting space, and a wide array of clean stainless-steel knives lined on a magnetic strip along one wall. The strip looked out of place, like something from a modern era intruding upon the past. Xander took a deep breath in through his nose and out through his mouth. The chemical scent of the foyer was still present, but beginning to fade, and here the room smelled like starch: the way too many potatoes smelled when crammed together in a dull, dry place.

"We have an on-staff cooking team that makes sure they're adhering to the most up-to-date information on a child's nutritional needs. Clara, our head chef, actually graduated from being a Nutritionalist after leaving here."

"You mean before coming here," Lisa corrected.

"Yes," Jeremy nodded, clasping his hands together. He waved a finger at her. "We should have you in as an English tutor."

There was something about the jibe that didn't seem light, but threatening, and Lisa brought Xander's arm closer to her. She smiled and nodded.

There was a laundry room off the kitchen that smelled of chemical detergent and made Xander sneeze. There were three washers and three dryers lined up along the wall, each one in the mid-range size. There was a washbasin with a large faucet on a hose dangling from the ceiling, an improvement on a holdover from when bedding was washed by hand. There were clotheslines stretched across the opposite wall that looked like they had not been use in decades.

They backtracked from the laundry back out to the kitchen, and through a small hallway was a dining room. It was large and had been designed for one long table, but was filled instead with several small circular ones, spaced equal distance apart. Each table was clean to a polished shine without a trace of dirt or crumbs or stain.

"Can I get you some coffee?" Jeremy asked, when he finished expositing about the enrichment programs they offered to supplement public education. He winked at Lisa. "Decaf for you, of course."

She shuddered.

"Yes," Xander said, authoritatively. His voice had lost the pleasant, plaintive tone of someone asking for a favor that it had had when he'd come in. "And I'd like to see the dormitories, please."

The smile slowly faded from Jeremy's lips. "I'm afraid we can't do that. Privacy."

"We don't want to see the rooms, just the floor. If that's okay."

"I'm sorry, but for the safety of the children --"

"There are no children upstairs," Xander said with

certainty, all trace of civility gone. He was staring at Jeremy now with eyes that were cold and dispassionate, and for his part Jeremy's facade was beginning to melt and become the same.

The two stood like that for a tense moment, standing across from each other in the dining room, like two gunslingers preparing to draw their weapons. It was like chess with no pieces and no words, both men taking the measure of the other silently, each waiting for the other to make the first move.

"Fine," Jeremy nodded, his perfect smile returning. Its presence now being the same as it had been before proved what Xander had suspected – that it had been manufactured and fake all along. He pointed with an open palm to a hallway that gave way to a stairwell. "Follow me."

The stairs were circular, spiraling up to the upper floor of each tower like the arc of a helix, the sort of design choice that made city planners today cringe. Once you were on the floor the hall stretched out before you on a slight incline and at a slight angle, allowing to get more space out of the available acreage. The rooms were lined off row on row, each one identical to the last save for stickers and posters and room numbers. Each door was painted the same pastel green that the flourishes of the mouldings on the first floor had been, with the walls being just a slight variation on the sunlight yellow.

Xander stopped in his tracks three feet from the stairwell, so quickly that Lisa didn't notice until the arm that clasped his pulled up taut. Jeremy was walking on in front of them, continuing his realtor-inspired commentary about the rooms and the arcs of the hall.

"What is it?" Lisa said from between clenched teeth, turning back to face Xander. "What's wrong?"

He was stiff, his nostrils flared.

Jeremy turned, and when his eyes found Xander's, he smiled. Not the game too-wide smile he'd been wearing before, but a wide, thin grin that pushed his cheeks up into his eyes. "Everything okay?"

"I've seen enough," Xander said, his voice hushed. He swallowed, his mouth thick with saliva, then spoke again: "We've seen enough."

"Oh, but you wanted to see the rooms. There's an extra communal kitchen just beyond the arc of the hall where the students can make cereal at night without coming downstairs, if they want to."

Xander took a step back, then turned, bringing Lisa with him by her hand. "We've seen enough."

Jeremy smiled and put his hands in his pockets, rocking forward with his thumbs out. "Well, do let me know what you decide," he said, his voice humming and pleased once more.

M

Xander gasped the second they were outside, his face red as though he'd been holding his breath for some time. He leaned over the rail that connected the street to the wide doors of Joucastle, took several long, shaking lungfuls of air, then threw up.

"What the fuck?" Lisa hissed, placing her hand against his back between the shoulders and rubbing.

He coughed, took a deep breath, then threw up again. This time it was nothing but coffee, that thick, sweet, brown bile that was hot again from being inside him and burned his nostrils like acid. It was good though; all he could smell was stomach acid now, and it was burning away the last remnants of Joucastle from his olfactory nerves.

"What's happening?" she asked again, glancing back through the doors to see if they were being watched.

"Death," Xander coughed, spitting up a large chunk of something from his gut. "That whole place stinks like death, Lisa."

She froze in place, her hand stopping against his back in mid-pat. "What?"

"The cleaner in the public place hides it, but there's blood there. Old blood, too much blood, too many... different bloods. A lot of different bloods and scents and *rot*." He turned to her, and when he did his pupils had grown to take up nearly his entire eye with blackness, leaving only a scant ring of white around their rims. "There's rotten blood coming up through the vents."

She swallowed, her hand shaking as she pulled it away from him.

CHAPTER TWENTY-ONE

Duncan laid the office box full of Shane employee files of the murder victims on the floor next to Tim's bed, then sat down in the chair next to it and ran his hands through his hair. He shook his nails against his scalp, made a frustrated sound, then pointed down at the box accusatorially. "This is useless. This... I could never work for business. You know why I can't work for business? Because this is useless." He kicked the box, not to harm it, but just for the catharsis of the kick itself.

Tim smiled a little. "Pedantic?"

"The definition of," Duncan said, taking the cover off the box. "They keep *everything* on people. They make people punch a clock when they go to break and when they go to lunch and when they take a shit, and there's..." he picked up a sheet and shook it angrily, "there's *reports* every week on if they spent too much time in shit-mode!"

Tim snorted and laughed.

"Yeah sure, funny. But I'm the one who's got to go through this crap to try and find anything useful, and how am I supposed to find anything useful when there *so much* there? Like, every point is buried by five other points." He put the file back. "Also, why do regular jobs keep track of sick days so closely? It's creepy."

Tim smirked again, and brought up his own digital copy of the personnel file.

Crowley sat across from Susan with her hands clasped before her in her lap. She had to clasp them to keep them from fidgeting, picking through her hair or running against the rim of her cup or twisting her rings. Constrained by each other was the only way to keep them out of trouble, she'd discovered.

"How'd you find the worksheets?" Susan asked, leaning forward and smiling.

"Good."

"Hated them?"

"Yeah," she smiled, nodding. "I went over them with my roommate though."

"That's good."

"She's been thinking of coming to therapy before she has the baby."

"That's good, too. I think all mothers should; I'm biased though, of course."

Crowley smiled.

"I can see if she can get an appointment if you like? We wouldn't have her meet with me though. Conflict of interest."

She started to fidget with her ring, stopped herself, and re-interlocked her fingers. "We'll see."

Susan nodded, leaning forward.

There was a long pause between them, and just as Susan looked as though she were about to break it, Crowley spoke up: "I think the fear of choosing started with my father." She winced as she spoke, spitting the words out fast at first, then slowing once the sentence began.

Susan put down her pen.

"He was a hard man. He'd been in the military when my mother met him, but he'd been out for a little while by the time I was born. You know that saying though, you can take the man out of the military... well, it's true. At least, it was true for him. My mother died when I was seven --"

"I'm sorry."

"-- And it was me and him then, and that was when everything changed. My mom, she was spontaneous -- at least I think she was. I have trouble remembering sometimes. But from what he says it was very much the flowerchild and the military-man stereotype. But when she left us it was all regiment, all the time. There wasn't... choice. It wasn't even like we were doing things his way, or doing things he wanted; it was like there was some unseen script that he was following too. It was just the way things were: there were orders to follow and we followed the orders."

Lisa came in through Tim's front door with her phone in hand and did not take off her shoes, finding Tim laying in his usual spot and Duncan sitting next to him. There were papers on the bed between them that Duncan seemed to be leafing through, a small disjointed huddle of them on his lap.

She paused a moment, hesitated, then continued in. "I

need help," she said, holding up her phone as if it was an explanation.

Tim furrowed his brow, wishing he could turn to see her as she found her way into view.

When she was next to the bed across from Duncan, she let out a long breath of air. Her face was flushed with sweat and her chest was heaving from heavy breathing. She picked up the phone and started to scroll through her apps. "It's Joucastle, there's something wrong there. Xander's there now." She held out the phone to face Tim. There was a web address printed in the notepad app. "Go here and he'll be able to stay in touch."

Tim tabbed open a browser and typed in the address as he was told.

Duncan slowly rose to his feet, taking the pile of papers from his lap and dropping them, without organization, back into the box they'd come from.

"He had this way of making it seem like you weren't doing things his way, you were just doing them the way they had to be done. I think that's the difference, that there's something there. Like, maybe if I'd grown up seeing him *make* the choices, I could have grown up to emulate that and make choices myself. But I never got to see the choosing process, things were just as they were... I never really noticed that they only seemed to ever benefit him, or be the way he wanted things to go, or be the way he wanted them to happen. Because they never seemed like choices; they seemed like... things. I don't know how to say it, but choice isn't the right word. I don't know what things seemed like, but choice didn't enter into it."

"Why aren't we waiting for backup?" Duncan asked. He'd come around to the front of the bed, so that the screens of Tim's computer were between them.

"We might be too late," Lisa winced. "There's kids."

"I get that," he said, gesturing as if holding out the opposing point of view. "But we should call. I'm going to --"

"It's been called," Tim barked, his voice harsh. "He's on it."

Duncan squinted, then nodded.

The browser window opened to a screen asking for a name, and he typed in TimLisa, then hit enter.

"I remember this one time, we went to see a movie. There was this huge wall with all the movies on it, I think it was my birthday, but I'm not sure – memories, right? Anyway, there's this huge wall and I'm like, twelve, but the movie I pick out is this cartoon that I would have been almost too old for. Not too old really, just a little. But he says, 'We're here to see this movie,' and whatever it is it's like this rated R film, I can't remember what it was. But it had lots of funny moments, but also a lot of violence and I was terrified of it. Maybe I wasn't twelve; maybe I was closer to ten.

"But he didn't say, 'I want to see this movie.' Like, it wasn't like I said, 'I want Choice A' and he said, 'Well, I want Choice B;' he said, 'We are here to see Choice B.' It was never framed as an equal choice, one versus the other, it was framed as like: 'I get that you want that, but that's not what's happening and there's nothing either of us can do to stop it.' I'm not sure he tried it."

"It sounds like he did," Susan said, calmly and sympathetically. She hadn't written any of it down.

"Yeah, I think maybe he did. It didn't occur to me until years later, though. Right before I moved out, I was dating this guy – this would have been late high school – and he was the same way. Bossy, but not saying what he wanted to do, just saying how things were going to be. And this one time the way he said things were going to be and the way Dad said things were going to be were different, and something just snapped on: This isn't the way it has to be."

Susan nodded.

"We're here," Tim typed, and the message came up on the screen with a speech balloon pointing to their avatar, the small, blue silhouette of a man.

"I left home less than a week later. I just did it... but it wasn't like a choice. I know it was, that I made it, but it doesn't *feel* like I had a choice. It just feels like it was... the way things had to be."

"We're here," came up on Xander's phone in green text on a black background.

He took a deep breath, then nodded, and typed, "I'm going in" before hitting send.

In front of him, Joucastle stood erect, towering into the dusty Los Angeles evening sky.

CHAPTER TWENTY-TWO

The side of Joucastle that faced the tenement building was dank and full of mold, the buildings that surrounded it never letting any light in to quell the gathering damp. Mold was a rarity in dry climates like Los Angeles, and when conditions were such that it could fester, it grew like a cancer: not the welcome fuzz of the forests he'd grown up around, but a thick, black, oily cancer that made every-thing slick and dangerous.

The space between the two buildings was so slight that Xander had to turn sideways to get in, and even now his chest scraped the stone wall and got a long smear of plaque across it for his trouble.

There were three windows at ground level, each with their lights out -- one at each end and one at the middle. He breathed as deep as he could in the constricted space, his chest not having the room to expand fully, and passed the first window as the shadow on Joucastle turned the hue of evening into the black of night.

When he reached the window he dropped down on all fours, like a linebacker doing up-downs. He had no room to brace himself and just let himself fall, catching the rocks with his chin, but saying nothing. He frowned and growled deep within his throat, internalizing it, feeling it add to the fire that was already building in the seat of his gut.

There was no light in the window and he heard nothing from inside it. He reached his arm back as far as he could and then slammed it forward, connecting the heel of his hand with the glass. The entire pane popped in, breaking into three large chunks when it hit the floor less than three feet below. It was a crawlspace.

"Fuck me," Xander cursed, then made his way into the space.

He came out in the kitchen, having squat his way beneath the leftmost wing of the building and the foyer until he reached a rickety staircase that was old but not disused. The starch scent of potatoes and carrots got stronger and stronger as he walked, and he realized that he was in a root cellar. He came out through one of the pantry doors that had been in the kitchen, among the stoves and fridges. His shirt was oily and black from the smut of the alley and the crawlspace. It didn't show for the black colour, but it did shine in the gloss from the light.

The kitchen was empty, just as it had been when Jeremy had walked them through. In fact, at no point during his crawl had Xander heard feet above him, nor did he hear any now. The walls were thick with shielding and soundproofing and asbestos and asbestos abatement foam... but he should have heard *something*.

He stepped from the kitchen to the laundry, and once

again that stench of powdered detergent hit him, blocking out anything else. He twitched and coughed, as low as he could, then stepped to the wall with three front-facing washers and dryers on it and glared at them.

The house seemed to go back forever, but this wall was solid and built as if it faced the outside, though they were nowhere near where the outside should be.

Joucastle was a large building, repurposed several times since its inception in the 1920s. It had started as an estate for a new-money stock trader and eventually became a speakeasy during prohibition.

The laundromat there was open twenty-four seven. It existed, primarily, through their proximity to Joucastle: they got the contract for the sheets, bedclothes, and garments.

He pulled open the metal door to the middle dryer. It still had stickers on the inside of the door, but the rest had been hollowed out, opening up fast to a long staircase lit by the glow of lamplight that spiraled down, just as the towers' had spiraled up, past the wall and down to the world below.

He lowered his eyes until they were tiny things in the center of his head. The smell of detergent that hid any other smells still burned him, but with the door open and the dank breeze coming up through from the cracks he could smell the dank and the rot and the metal that the detergent had been meant to hide. He glowered, then took out his phone and took a picture of the hidden door, sending it to the chat. He paused while it was sent, ran his tongue along the back of his teeth, then ducked down to enter the stairwell.

The stairwell was sparsely lit, its corkscrew design making it impossible to see more than the few feet illuminated by the faintest glow of the lamps until the stone corners blocked their path. The smell of the laundry was far behind him now, and all his nostrils could find was the putrid fried-chicken smell of old sweat. There were layers of it, layers upon layers, decades of sweat that had fallen off the bodies marched down into the depths of this place and absorbed by the stone steps.

His pupils enlarged to take in as much of the surroundings as he could, but there was nothing but stone and the occasional rat. The rats were fat with sloshy water weight, and stank of the coppery tang of blood. The further he descended, the stronger the stench was, hitting him in waves as his stomach flipped inside him. It was stronger than any time he'd ever smelled it before: stronger than any time he'd bled until he thought there was no blood left in him, than when it had caked onto him and dried there and gotten hard like a sick shielding scab.

The stairway opened in front of him, finishing their decent and becoming a long hall. It was wide and stretched off for at least one hundred feet, and must have gone under the street and beyond to the laundromat, he realized.

He stepped into this new room with trepidation. There were a few lights, and what he saw were the outlines of large geometric shapes, stacked high against the walls and looming forward, as if he was stepping inside a life-size model of the Lego buildings he'd made on his living room map.

He cursed, then took out his phone again and turned on the flash. He took two pictures, then looked at them: no humans, and the shapes were crates.

"Rum runners," he mouthed, remembering the building's history. He pressed to send the photos to Tim and Lisa again. The hourglass spun, then stopped, and produced the message: NO SIGNAL. "Fuck you," he cursed, shutting the hinge and shoving it back into his pocket. He took a deep breath, cast one glance back towards the stairwell, then pressed on toward the end of the hall.

The barrels and crates loomed overhead like gargoyles, staring down at him, the faded print stamped on their sides long ago making leering, taunting faces at him.

The hall turned again and abruptly dropped a foot and twisted to the side, like a funhouse mirror version of itself. It twisted and righted and twisted again in a way structures shouldn't, the ceiling arching down and cracking in places.

Los Angeles was prone to earthquakes.

He shook his head and turned to leave, when he heard something far at the other end of the tunnel, so far and so tainted by echoes that it may as well have been coming from underwater.

It was the sound of a child crying. That unmistakable sound of sobbing and wailing and trying to keep quiet but failing that only a child could accomplish. His eyes lowered again, and he stepped down to the lower level of the hall.

"Hey."

Xander turned around abruptly and came face-to-face with that toothy, gummy smile that had greeted him in the Joucastle foyer. The white of the teeth were visible in the dark for only an instant, before there was a flash of something thin and metal and sharp. There was pressure at his neck and the world turned sideways. Pain exploded against the side of his face and he found his mouth full of dirt.

He started to stand, but whatever had hit him did so again, then a third time, and then in the stomach.

There were many more strikes, but Xander was not awake to feel them.

CHAPTER TWENTY-THREE

Erica Shane ran sharp nails through her hair scratching at the scalp with such ferocity she may have made it bleed. She did this for a full minute as she stamped her way across her father's penthouse toward the bay window on its opposite side, then transitioned into shaking her hair loose from the elastic that held it in place. She let out a frustrated huff, leaned both palms against the glass, and stared out at the city that existed between her two thumbs.

Her father, Arthur Shane, entered the room, his cheeks flush. He went straight for the island in the middle of his kitchen. He pulled out a bottle of wine and a glass from the dispensary in it and poured himself an ample glass, then drank it, tilting the glass back more and more until the entirety of it had disappeared into his mouth. He gasped when he took the glass away, then started to pour again.

Erica turned to him, scowling. "Could you not?"

He glared at her, leaning forward on the island to catch his breath. "That was a massacre," he said, his voice thick with burst capillaries.

"Phrasing, Father."

He took a mouthful of his drink again, then scrolled past the stocks app on his phone. "Our stock has dropped another eight points," he said, almost without emotion. He rubbed his thumb against his right eyelid, cursed, then sat at the stool that was at the island.

She pushed off from the glass and walked over to the island, her hair falling over one shoulder in a brown-and-purple heap. She took the glass from in front of him, drank a small mouthful herself, then placed it back within his reach. "The board disapproved my request for funds into an a PR-spin campaign."

He pursed his lips and nodded. "Do you think they're going to post no-confidence motion on us?"

She nodded curtly. "I do."

He sighed, then filled his glass again.

CHAPTER TWENTY-FOUR

Lisa sat on the last inch of her seat, hunched forward with the second knuckle of her left forefinger clasped between her teeth, white with strain. She was tapping her foot without realizing it, the angle she was sitting at triggering an unconscious bounce in her leg muscles.

The patio door was open and Duncan was standing outside near the barbeque, his hands straddling his hips in a way she had only ever seen police do.

Tim wasn't – *couldn't* – make any motion to display or disperse his anxiety, but it showed in how there were no windows open on his multi-screen display, save for the one which displayed the chat window between he and Xander.

It had the picture of the tunnel hidden behind the dryer that Xander had sent on screen, along with three return messages they'd sent, but no responses.

Lisa leaned over and looked at the chat window for the third time in five minutes. "It's been too long," she said, her voice quavering. She looked at the timestamp on the picture. "It's been over an hour."

There was blood.

That was the first thing Xander realized when consciousness returned to him, before he could move, before he could speak, before he could see or think: he registered the coppery tang of blood, on him, in him, and all around him.

"Erm," he grunted, feeling his pulse quicken and find its way to his temples, where it met some obstruction and began to pound. His head throbbed and he felt the telltale muscular squirt that most people didn't experience and live to tell about, of his own blood finding a break in the flesh that covered the back of his head and forcing its way out. When he opened his eyes, everything around him looked black and smelled like copper and mold. "Fuck me," he mumbled.

"Believe me, that's tempting."

His eyes shot open fully, his pupils adjusting to the low light of the cavern. It smelled the same as the tunnel that he'd last been conscious in had: that same stink of old hops and barley and black mold that came from alcohol kept too long and in the wrong conditions, but now it was joined by the harsh stink of ozone and lamp oil. He was against a rock, he realized, the black he saw not the black of pitch but the black of granite, the flickering light from behind him glistening off its slick surface. He turned slowly in the direction the voice, melodic and musical, had come from.

She was crouching over him in a way a woman wearing a dress like hers typically didn't. It was a red dress with long slits up either leg, the fabric draping down and hanging in the arc she'd formed between her legs. She wasn't wearing shoes, he realized with an odd fixation, staring at manicured toes that stood atop jagged, sloping rock. Her hair, long and blonde, fell down over her shoulders in tumbling curls, just as it had on the security footage he had twice seen her on now.

She smiled at him as their eyes met, her crimson lips parting to reveal white, perfect teeth. "Hello," she beamed.

He lunged forward at her but came up short, his arms pulling tight and screaming at him when they met their mark. "Fuck!" he yelled, turning back and finding that his wrists were bound with cuffs to a thick metal peg that came out of the wall. He recognized it from when his father had worked in the mines when he was young, as the sort of strong anchor used to descend a deep tunnel. He pulled on it twice nonetheless and it would not budge.

"I got those from a police captain in Vegas who used to get me to use them on him and fuck him until he bled," she said, cocking her head toward the handcuffs. Her voice was pleasant and hummed, despite what she was saying. "If he couldn't break them during what I did to him, they can't be broken."

Xander gasped, the metal of the cuff snapping a bone in his right thumb as he gave it one last, forceful tug. He made several attempts at taking lungfuls of air, but found the oxygen was thick with metal and dust and particles of filth.

He turned back to her, his gaze rueful, finally seeing behind her.

They were near the bottom of a steep drop that came down twenty feet from the tunnel he'd been in. He could see the mouth of it above now, the last of its rail track sticking out over the lip of its edge. From there it descended in slopes and valleys, with edges carved out like bleachers in rims. There were tool marks and long gouges in rings around the edge, some haphazard and some etched into ornate swirling patterns.

The drop continued for about ten feet below him, ending in a large stone that seemed too large and thick to obliterate and had instead been etched with swirls as well, intermingled with primitive carvings of creatures on four legs – the effect being that they were dogs with misshapen heads floating on Van Gough's winds along some sky that seemed very far away from down here.

There were children sitting along the edges of the cavern, their feet dangling haphazardly over the steep drop to the rock below. They watched with plain faces devoid of thought, all their eyes glued to him, or rather, to the blonde woman that sat crouched in front of him. None of them twitched or moved or fiddled, in the way that most children that age did. Not that they were all young – the vast majority, but not all – but they were all under eighteen; this he knew even though some of them had the worn, wrought expressions of people who had lived till at least their thirties.

Xander saw a brunette girl with blue eyes and plump cheeks looking down from a perch ten feet above him, and recognized her as eight year old Ava Miller, one of the first he'd pinned to his map. She'd grown thinner since the last photo he'd seen of her, and there was a long burn along one of her cheeks. There were more he could recognize – all of them, he suspected – but his eyes kept drawing back to the blonde woman who was smiling at him garishly, all the eyes of all the children on she.

She took his face in her hand and drew him forward until their noses touched. "My name is Celena," she grinned, her voice sweet and salty all at the same time. "What's yours?"

There were children close to her, so close they made Xander uncomfortable. They were clothed in shirts too small for them and dotted in filth, and each of them had visible scabs: the sort that lingered and kept getting re-opened and became a puss-filled gangrenous sore by the time it was dealt with. Celena turned from Xander and walked to the nearest group of children, a group of four that looked to have a mean age of about ten, and one larger boy who seemed much older.

One of the smaller children coughed and spat. Xander thought he recognized the older of them from an old police file photo, but couldn't be sure. If it was the same child that had gone missing all those years ago, he had gained weight in the weirdest, most implausible way possible: becoming chubby and saggy in the cheeks while slender and withered in the extremities. It seemed impossible, like a human caricature of a hot-air balloon, or a pear standing on its head.

Celena brought her nails to him and ran them over his skin, then up through his hair, in a way that looked similar to that which Lisa had touched Tim, but was different – it was one of those rare human interactions where intent shone through, and in this the intent was *possession*. In one fluid motion she had told Xander everything he needed to know about her relationship to these children.

"Jeremy," she said.

The administrator of Joucastle appeared immediately into Xander's limited frame of view, holding a short blade out to her. It glistened in the low light of the cavern and shone a light green from the tip of the blade to the climax of the handle, which was carved to look insectile, with one large winged bug taking up the majority of the grip.

She smiled at Xander, still running her hands through the teen's hair. He was an older teen, near the cusp of manhood, he thought.

His fogged head cleared in an instant and he got a sudden flash of inspiration, realizing what was happening. He pulled forward against his restraints and screamed, "No!"

There was a photograph of the dead body. It was a young adult male with acne scars dotting the edges of his hair line, along with a straight red line through the left side of his neck, stretching from his collar bone to nearly the base of his chin.

Celena pulled the boy's hair back and exposed the nape of his neck, lowering the jade blade to just touch the supple flesh it found there.

"No!" he screamed again, his voice shaking into a growl as his eyes started to flare, becoming more and more dark and black. He hauled on his chain with a solid, forceful tug that snapped his thumb's major phalange before it righted itself again. He cursed and growled and fought, pulling so hard he felt like the flesh of his arm would tear loose and continuing to pull anyway.

Celena kept her gaze leveled at him, tilting her head to

one side and letting her hair move and flow with gravity.

At the last possible moment, Xander remembered the boy's name: he was Lawrence Reative, and his grandparents had come from Austria after the Second World War

Celena said seven words in a language Xander had never heard before, one that seemed to come as naturally to her as English. She pressed the sharp blade into Lawrence's neck just above his collarbone and it slid in as though it were butter, blood pouring out in a way that couldn't be mimicked on television or movies: it was something that when you saw it in real life, your brain didn't quite know what to do with.

Lawrence was staring ahead at Xander too, his eyes dead even before he died, not reacting to the blade at his throat in the slightest.

"Fuck, NO!" he yelled again, giving one last powerful shove, bracing off the balls of his feet, before slipping and falling to the ground in a stir of dust.

The children surrounding him watched him, most without expression.

Celena pulled back Lawrence's hair even further, and the slit in his neck made the extended motion possible. She bore in the blade and brought it up through his throat, withdrawing it with a flick of her wrist when she felt it connect with the bone of his chin. She turned and hung him over the precipice of the cavern, his head tilted back at an obscene, impossible angle as the blood spurted and poured out of him, dropping to the stenciled floor below and splashing there in huge waterfall staccato sounds.

Xander opened his dirt-filled eyes and saw the children staring down at him, their tiny faces suddenly alight from a bluish glow from below, the way campfire instructors put flashlights under their chips to exaggerate their features. He turned back in time to see Celena drop the body of the young man and hear it land a moment later against the rock and the dust surrounding the ground. She was backlit now as light poured up from the cavern floor, each of the etchings there and along the wall glowing an ethereal blue and pulsing again and again before eventually fading and going out.

He swallowed hard as she turned her attention back to him, bringing her blade up to waist-height. "It's a death cult."

CHAPTER TWENTY-FIVE

"It's been too long," Duncan said for the third time. He was standing in the patio door with his cigarette lit between his lips. Every puff he took made him wretch and his eyes water, and yet he also seemed to be craving it, running his hands through his hair and turning his head skyward with each suck at the filter. "This has gone FUBAR; it must have."

Lisa was sitting in her seat next to Tim's bed with both her hands clasped before her, her elbows resting on her knees, as though she were in prayer. She shook -- and every so often, a tear slipped loose from her eye as the sight of the blank text-response screen just stared at her unemotionally.

There was a second window open on the screen now, a large digital phone keypad. Tim punched in the number for Xander's burner cell again, and his speakers produced half a ring before a robotic voice announced, "We're sorry, this number is not in service."

"Call for backup," Duncan said, motioning to the app on the screen. He took out his own phone and started thumbing through his own applications. He paced the room as he spoke, his tone taking on a commanding tenor Tim had not heard in some time. "I'll get federal backup, you contact – where was he from? Ten? – LAPD10 and get them to send every motherfucker they have down to that place, but tell them *no sirens*. Last thing we need is these fuckers getting antsy and --" He stopped.

Lisa stared at Tim with wide eyes, her mouth a small thing that was covered up by her praying hands completely. He was looking back at her, his eyebrows upturned and worried.

Duncan looked from Lisa to Tim, and then back again, his thumb hovering over the call icon on his phone. All at once his expression changed from blankly contemplative to one thick with anger and spite, his lip curling as he turned back to Tim and stepped toward him. "You son of a bitch, he's not PD is he?"

Tim swallowed, turning his gaze to Duncan.

"You fucking hypocrite!" he yelled. He grabbed the rail at the edge of the bed and shook it once for effect, not moving it. His cheeks were livid now, all traces of the concern he'd expressed a moment ago gone. "Fucking rat hypocrite!"

"This isn't helping," Lisa commanded, standing to her full height.

"You sit down right now," Duncan barked, thrusting a finger at her. "You're damn lucky you're not under arrest. You might well be, so don't push your goddamn luck."

She fumed at that, nostrils flaring. "He's still in there!"

"Six months," Duncan continued, turning his accusing finger at Tim as though she hadn't responded. "Six months suspension because of you and your mouth and your goddamn bleeding heart for a fucking piece of garbage CI, and what are you doing the second I see you again? Sending a civilian in to be your legs."

"You're right," Tim said, his voice a small thing in the back of his throat.

"Pardon?"

"You're right. You're right and I... I don't have anything to say. I don't have a leg to stand on."

Duncan winced, his sneer twitching, then tried to snarl again, and eventually let out a rueful laugh. He leaned forward onto the rail of Tim's bed, chuckled, then turned back to face him. "You said it."

"Please," Lisa begged, stepping forward and putting her hand over Duncan's. "Please help us."

Duncan looked at her hand, small and white on his constantly calloused and sunburnt leathery hand. He looked from it to her, working his jaw from side to side as he thought. After a moment, he broke off, moved to the couch, and grabbed his coat. "Fuck it."

Crowley sat alone in the center of the Los Angeles city map that was spread out over her living room floor. There was a box of photographs in front of her, tattered and weathered badly. She picked through them one by one, being in none of them herself. They were Xander's photos, and she flipped through them like files in a cabinet until she found one of him: a younger him that wasn't really him at all anymore, with three of his friends.

She took it and played it between her fingers, flapping it back and forth, then turned and looked around the cluttered mess of the room and the photos of dead children strewn about everywhere.

Xander screamed, so long and so loud that his voice broke, the pitch altering rapidly from a bellow into a high pitched wail.

His shirt was in tatters around him; Celena had ripped it off him in strips, pulling at each with sudden, jolting tugs that tore at the flesh on his back before they ripped and came loose. What was left of his shirt clung to him around the arms like flares.

She had marvelled at first at how pale his skin was – how gaunt. She had brought her sharp fingernails to the flesh of his pectoralis muscles, each sharp implement depressing the skin just to point of puncturing and stopping short of it, dragging her nails all over the outlines of his breast and abdomen, leaving long white trails of distressed flesh behind her.

She had driven the cold tip of her blade through the flesh of his central plexus as though it were tissue paper, hollowing out a hole and then pushing her fore and middle fingers in until they were all but completely within him. She wriggled and wormed there like a pubescent boy finding his first feel and unsure of what to do or where to go, her hand flapping about in the wet sludge that came out of him like a fishtail. Dark blood fell from the hole she'd made in him, much larger and less cleanly circular than a bullet hole, the inky red pouring down over his stomach and making it look like a slab of ground beef, ready for dissecting.

He screamed again, breaking eye contact with her and thrusting his head skyward with enough force to crimp it, though he could not feel it. The brain had a gating mechanism for pain, he'd learned long ago. It prioritized severe pain and ignored any other, and right now his brain was focused on, exclusively, the writhing, wriggling fingernails that had slipped past his ribs and were now scratching playfully at the folds on his lungs.

In concentric circles along the edge of the cavern, children watched, some of them showing signs of being disturbed or distressed... but most of them showing no emotion on their faces at all, as though they had seen this sort of torture a dozen times before. They likely had.

"You're so *tight*," she said with humor, laughing to herself. She pulled her fingers from him and he heard the wet suckle of suction as his flesh turned itself inside out like a glove to try and keep her.

"Nn-guh," he managed to grunt, his eyes alternating between bulging wide and clamped shut in equal measure.

She grabbed him by the face again, forcing him to look at her. "That's it; this is always better with audience participation," she hummed, that voice like the warm of spring in his ears, the perfect anathema to the cold shoots of pain bolting down his nerves from his central plexus. She held him like that for a moment, smiling with her lips close to his, then allowed him to drop to the rocky floor once more. "Tease."

He opened his eyes and could barely see more than

stark white from the impact his skull had made. As he watched, his blood mingled with the dried pools of it in the rocky floor he lay out, joining with a dozen different gelatinous pools of it that had gathered and stank and begun to rot over weeks and months. He gasped, struggling to fill his lungs.

Celena turned back to him with teeth that were stained with the red of him now. She grabbed him by the shoulder and forced him back against the wall, pinching the tendon that connected his neck to his shoulder so hard that it bled. "You're a fun toy, but I'm just about --"

She stopped, her fingers floating over the hole she'd just made in him, finding nothing but smooth, gaunt flesh, slick with blood. She pushed the blood away in time to see the last of it, the hole she'd widened, well over and inch shriveling to the size of a pinprick and then disappearing in a spurt of blood and puss.

She squinted and turned back to him, finding that his eyes were deep, deep black from their pupils all the way to their outer rim.

"My turn," he growled, his voice thick and angry.

CHAPTER TWENTY-SIX

Xander pulled on the cuffs that bound him to the wall, hearing the bone that connected his thumb to the rest of his hand make a forceful wet snap again, maintaining eye contact with Celena all the while as she stepped away, stopping at the edge of the precipice.

Several of the children were leaning forward now, this new development one they hadn't previously seen. Jeremy had appeared behind two, Desmond and Brittney, looming behind them and looking down as Xander thrust on his chains again and again, each time progressing a millimetre more than the time before and accompanied by a wet, sucking snap.

With one last pull, he yanked his arm free, tearing away a great strip of flesh and leaving his thumb and fingers dangling, a useless maw that was already beginning to stitch itself back together before their eyes. Celena watched this with an expression somewhere between awe and horror, stepping back a pace, and the blood gushing from Xander's arm ceased to be red and flowing and began to be black and tar-like, bubbling up and sticking to him like tar exiting an industrial tube.

Four long claws erupted from the fingers on his free hand as the black blood and putrid bile that came out of him in swirling animated snakes clung to him and coated his bare chest anew. He turned the talons back and pressed them through the flesh of his remaining bound hand, the blood and the blade providing the leverage to slip free at last. He caught himself as he hit the floor, his eyes bulging with blackness that had started to be red in its middle and the tar staggered, coating him finally. "I might never have seen something like you, but you've never seen anything like me," he growled, then leapt forward.

He connected his fist full-force with her jaw and heard the sound of blood and muscle dispersing, the moist snap of bone been torn out from between muscle and sinew after a forceful impact.

He screamed.

He pulled his hand away, the hand that had not been broken in his escape from her cuffs. Two of his fingers were missing, the impact of hitting Celena's face with such force having shattered them. The rest of his hand was a crippled maw of spurting black flesh, white bone shoving its way out from inside it so quickly that the black bile of the womb had difficulty keeping up with it.

He cursed and turned back to Celena, clutching his useless hand.

Her face was undamaged, save for the bright smear of red lipstick he'd pushed onto her cheeks, the only evidence that he'd actually connected with her. She smiled and tilted her head in that same way she had a moment before, her blonde hair the only clean thing in the sullen, dank cavern. "You're interesting," she said, then drove her blade forward.

The jade short-sword sunk through his central plexus where her fingers had been before and jutted out the other side. His brain was a gaggle of warning and painful alarms as he felt his healing factor pinch and try desperately to shove the blade back out, to no avail. He spurted blood and realized she'd punctured a lung.

She spun him around using the handle of the blade like a marionette handle, until his feet were just touching the edge of the fall to the cavern's edge. She drew back her other hand and backhanded him with such force that he was pushed off of the blade. He flew for a moment, her force so great that he defied gravity. He had just begun to feel the pull of inertia dragging him back to earth when his shoulder connected to the other side of the cavern wall, with enough force to send jagged spurs of bone out into the surrounding muscle.

He tried to scream, but vomited instead, falling and tumbling off the jagged edges of the cavern until he reached the etched stone below. The blackness that had only come from him like an armor a moment ago now hung from him like loose threads, dangling and trying to grip his skin for dear life. His bones tried to knit themselves, each slide and motion of them sending spasms of pain throughout him that he could only ignore for the screaming pain coming from everywhere else, bowel and bladder voiding themselves and preparing for the worst.

She landed next to him, her blade in hand.

When he looked up at her, she was smiling, her pupils the large, unblinking pupils of a porcelain doll.

CHAPTER TWENTY-SEVEN

Lisa slammed into the solid glass door of Joucastle, hammering the push handle with both palms, but still coming up solid, the full weight of her body not budging the glowing wall of light that stood erect against the gathering dark of the night.

She pushed it twice more, frantic, each time making more and more noise. "It's locked!" she yelled, turning back to Duncan as he finished his ascent of the stairs.

He raised his gun and fired two shots through the glass, splintering it and turning it into a spider-webbed mess before he connected his boot with it, sending it shattering inward in a long rectangle of sharp chaos that stretched out over Joucastle's tiled foyer like a shadow.

Lisa screamed when the shots came, clutching both her ears and her hair at the same time.

"It's open now," he said, stepping under the push handle and into the facility. "Try and keep up."

She cursed, then followed.

Arthur Shane sat in his penthouse alone, the only light in the room filtering up from the street. When he'd started with his wine, it had been midday and turning the lights on hadn't been needed, and he hadn't adjusted as evening fell.

There were two empty wine bottles next to him, and a third in his hand. He had chosen to forego the bottle this time, and was drinking the velvety red wine straight from the neck.

"The board is going to have a no confidence vote," he said, speaking into the darkness, before taking a long swig of his wine.

He finished the bottle before heading to bed.

"You don't seem to want to *stop* bleeding, do you?" Celena smiled, noting the way the black womb-flesh tried to knit the stab wounds she made closed the second she withdrew the blade. The blade was black now with his innards, the small trail of crimson swirling its way down through the ink.

Xander's eyes were swelling shut and his lip hung open, unable to close and dropping liquid of every colour and texture from its orifice. His vision was dotted by white dots that had deep black shadows. The black tar that protected him had been driven back from his face, revealing the pale and sickly man beneath, cheeks greened and reddened from popped blood vessels and far, far too many times vomiting.

She pressed her lips to his and then opened her mouth and bit, tearing away a chunk of his lip while laughing.

She pushed him forward, gripping him by the hair and extending his neck out over the center of the image they stood upon. "I wonder," she said, then brought her green blade up again. He tried to move, but his limbs refused to obey him, and she sunk her blade deep into his neck.

His blood hit the floor in splotching, dark spurts.

The floor began to glow.

"I think I hear something," Lisa whispered, tip-toeing her way through the long, wide hall. It stretched on for at least a hundred feet. Each of her steps was tentative and anxious; she expected any one of her footfalls to find something she didn't want it to.

Duncan raised his gun to eye level, pointing it towards the beam of light at the end of the hall. "I hear it too. It sounds like... kids. Like kids talking."

There were a few lights, and what he saw were the outlines of large geometric shapes, stacked high against the walls and looming forward.

"What is all this?" she asked in a hushed voice.

"Looks like a prohibition highway. Must have been scrapped hard, because if not the triads would have used it for transporting meth for sure." The hall turned and abruptly dropped a foot and twisted to the side, then righted and twisted and righted and twisted again in a way structures shouldn't, the ceiling arching down and cracking in places. "...Or they were scared of quakes."

"Rightly so by the looks of things," she said, looking at the floor with her lip curled in disgust.

"He can't have gone this way," Duncan said, shaking

his head. "We must have missed an entrance in the distillery."

A scream rang out from down the hall, and Duncan raised his gun and jumped down the drop to the shaky floor below without hesitation. Lisa followed, taking care to find her way down the incline.

The floor beneath Xander glowed a fierce blue light, so bright it had almost transcended the spectrum and become as bright and white as the midday sun. It blared at him and seared him, so hot that it burned his cheeks and the exposed flesh under his chin. Blood flowed freely from him onto the cavern floor and he screamed, as long as loud as he could. Every time the blood's rate threatened to cease, Celena reached her blade around again and cut a new slit, fighting his womb-organ's efforts to keep him whole.

She was saying something, softly, in a tongue he couldn't understand. The words were harsh, with the ashes and hard-H sounds of Old English and the Middle East, with the quickness and elongated A's of eastern languages, but was neither. Was nowhere close to anything he had ever heard before, its speed and tenor seeming to go on at no end.

"Ok'Tid weet may'd ream der g've sing lad crme yorr ne'r ri das end til unthe thew morf fo e'er dea owo wtub how tow."

A bright light erupted not below him from the stone, but next to him: a shimmering break in reality that filled the room with the putrid stench of bile and rot the moment it appeared.

A deep, rumbling growl filled the air, and for a moment, Xander thought he could see movement just beyond the light.

A gunshot rang out suddenly, and Celena jolted back as though she'd been punched in the face.

Xander fell to the ground, his palms landing on the glowing blue stone and sizzling in pain. He rolled away, and when his flow of blood was taken away, the growling light shimmering in the air where he had been winked out and the ground began to cease its glow.

He looked up and saw Lisa and Duncan standing at the upper mouth of the cavern, Duncan's gun still aimed at Celena and smoking.

CHAPTER TWENTY-EIGHT

Celena rose up from the ground, a dark bruise along her cheek and jaw where Duncan's bullet had struck, glaring at Xander as he struggled to remain on his feet.

"Get everyone out of here!" he yelled hoarsely to Lisa and Duncan, without tearing his eyes away from Celena's cautious narrowing of the gap between them.

"Come on!" Lisa yelled, grabbing the nearest child by the shoulder and pulled them to their feet. "We have to go!"

The children seemed to snap out of their blank stares down at Celena, heads turning all as one in waves. They were like ducks following the duck in front of them in a line behind the mother fowl: each time one got up and followed Lisa's urging to venture along the ridge to safety, the next few in line would notice the absence and turn their heads. Their eyes remained dead and dull at first, but there was something about Lisa that warmed them: the motherly glow and the slight bulge of her middle, perhaps.

"Come on!" Duncan shouted. He had moved down to

the level below the entrance he had come through, moving slowly and carefully, making sure to keep the barrel of his gun trained on the action happening below. He moved further as more and more children moved and vacated, and by now had reached the part of the cavern whose etched runes still glowed a faint neon blue. "Drew, it's time to go!"

Xander heard Duncan as though he were underwater, some small part of him acknowledging that the agent had used his real name. Blood filled his ears and limited the amount he could hear above the gurgling, moistness of his heartbeat, and all his attention was focused on the woman circling him along the edge of the area she'd carved in the center of the cavern, her lower half coated in blood she'd taken from him, and from others.

Celena smiled, the smear of her lipstick making it seem as though her lips went too far up her cheeks when she did, turning it into a Glasgow Smile. Her teeth were round rocks with an even, uncanny amount of space between them. She was closer than she had been, refusing to take her eyes off of Xander's, slowly closing the distance between them.

Duncan raised his gun again, tracking the steady motions Celena was taking around the center of the room and taking aim at the side of her head.

"No!" Jeremy screamed, appearing from under the ledge and lashing out at Duncan. He had a long, hooked stick – like a scythe – and he hooked Duncan's legs out from under him, dragging him down to his level.

Duncan landed on his back with a full, painful thud and cursed loudly, his vision going white around the edges.

"You cannot defeat Mistress Celena!" he yelled, his voice thick with venom and rage. He held his stick with both hands, each gripping and loosening furtively, anxious and filled with adrenaline. "None of this will work, none of it!" He raised the stick high again.

A rock collided with the side of Jeremy's head, splitting the skin at its temple and bisecting his face with blood. He dropped the stick, and it fell to a level further down and then kept tumbling down the slope toward Xander and Celena. He turned his angry, gritted teeth to see Lisa standing several levels above him, already holding a second rock.

"You get the fuck away from him," she said bitterly.

Celena lunged forward, grabbing Xander by the neck before his swollen eyes could register what was happening. He tried to cough, but her grip was too tight, wedging his windpipe shut as she slammed him against the wall of the cavern.

"It's been so long since I met someone like me," she cooed, bringing the sharp fingers of her opposing hand up and puncturing the new flesh of his abdomen with them. The bruise on her cheek from the gunshot was growing, seemingly by the second, half her face now tinged with purple.

He tried to scream but couldn't.

"I'd begun to think there wasn't hope for it but: here you are. And here I am. And now everything's going to be right again -- you'll see." Her hand was inside him, among his small intestines. His lips were turning dark blue. "Yooooou'll see."

Lisa threw another rock at Jeremy as he tried to move closer to Duncan, who had rolled onto his side and was coughing, trying to regain himself. Jeremy dodged it as he had the second and third stones, able to see them coming now. The blood from the gash on his forehead had found its way to his neck now, soaking his collar.

"Cunt!" he yelled, as he was forced away from Duncan by another stone. "I will not have this!"

A stone slammed against the side of his head, near where Lisa's had struck. It was small and he stumbled, bringing a hand to his face and gripping the mangled flesh he found there.

Luka, Desmond, and Brittney were standing with several other children on the ledge down from Lisa, each of them holding their own stones as Desmond picked up another to replace the one he had hit Jeremy with.

"Again!" Desmond yelled, and four of them launched their rocks at once, too many for Jeremy to dodge. Two hit him and he stumbled, falling to one knee.

"Hey fucktard!" Lisa yelled, and when he turned in her direction, a large stone left her hand with such speed that it seemed to teleport the distance between them, connecting with the bridge of his nose with a large spurt of blood.

He screamed.

Duncan arose to his feet and coughed twice, Jeremy near him at his knees, clutching his face. "Wish I had time to do this right," he said under his breath. He grabbed Jeremy by the back of the head and forced it forward into the cavern wall, finally falling into unconsciousness. "I'll read you your damn rights when you wake up."

He turned up and locked eyes with Lisa, whose hair clung to her with sweat in the low blue glow of the cavern, and nodded. She nodded back, then turned and motioned for Luka and the other children to come to her.

Duncan checked his gun and then raised it, turning it back down towards the carnage below.

Xander was striking at Celena with open hands, each blow weaker than the last as he felt every ounce of oxygen and energy ebb out of him.

"Don't go, not yet," Celena cooed, taking her hand out of him and stroking the side of his head, smearing it with his own blood and innards. "The fun has just started."

"Drew!" Duncan screamed, at the top of his lungs. "Kick off!" He raised his gun skyward.

Summoning every ounce of strength he had left, Xander raised his feet and pressed them against Celena's chest and pushed, breaking their connection and sending her back toward the center of the room.

"Don't you dare--" she started, her voice shaking with anger.

Duncan fired four shots into the air in rapid succession, only stopping his squeeze when he felt the hammer of his gun connect with nothing and click.

The stalactite Duncan had been aiming for came loose from the ceiling of the cavern and fell, striking the paths carved and worked on for years on the way down. Lisa screamed and the few remaining children in the cavern yelled as the rock fell, finally landing between Xander and Celena and cutting one off from the other.

Xander gasped for air and got a lungful of dust, but still gasped for more.

Celena screamed as more rocks started to fall: not from pain or from fear, but from pure, unbridled anger. The stones the stalactite had slammed loose on its decent started their own decent, some falling rapidly to the cavern floor and shattering the etched ground, others tumbling down the steep incline and starting avalanches that brought grit and gravel with them.

"Drew!" Duncan yelled.

Xander turned and saw Duncan was on the level above him now, holding his hand down to him. He took it and was pulled up, and both men made their way hurriedly to the top of the cavern as it crumbled around them, the impact of each stone falling shaking loose three more.

Eventually they stopped hearing Celena's screaming.

CHAPTER TWENTY-NINE

"What the hell did this?" Tim yelled as he watched Lisa lay Xander on his couch. His eyes were all but swollen shut, the lids like purple baseballs sticking out the front of his head. His lips were in equally bad shape and one of his ears had begun to cauliflower from pressure. Tim aimed his computer's camera at him, watching as Lisa tried to wash the blood from him, using one of the sponges his nurses kept for him.

"I don't know," Lisa said, pushing the hair out of Xander's face and turning him toward her. "I just... I don't know. But whatever she was, she's dead now."

"There's no way she's dead," Xander croaked, trying to get up.

She held him down by his chest. "Don't talk, don't talk."

"She's still out there," he said, blood foaming from his mouth. "I've never faced anything like that before, and it's definitely still out there."

Jeremy sat in the holding cell at LAPD12, blood drying along the left side of his face in almost a straight line.

Janet Nesbit looked at him over the CCT camera feed in Homicide12, having rolled the portable television over to her desk. She and Duncan both leaned against it and watched as he turned his head from one side of the cell to the other, almost like a tick.

"Should we get him medical attention?" Janet asked, taking a sip of her coffee.

"He's fine," Duncan said bluntly, glowering at the screen. His back felt like one large bruise.

"Protocol says --"

"Fuck 'em. You have no idea what this little fuck put me through. Honestly? Fuck him."

Janet raised an eyebrow to him, then nodded and smiled, cocking her head. "Okay. Fuck 'em it is."

The light flicked in the detention cell.

Duncan stood up. "What the fuck was that?"

"Power surge. It happens all the time; it's an old system."

It flickered again, for longer this time

Jeremy stood up and turned to face the camera in the corner of the room, locking eyes with Duncan even though they were separated by several floors. He smiled.

The camera feed blinked out.

Lisa winced as she entered her apartment, the act of getting her leg over the archway tremendous. She hissed, pressed her hand against her stomach, and then was inside.

"Where were you?" Crowley asked, hopping down

off the kitchen counter and stepping over to meet her. "Where's Xander?"

"He's at Tim's," Lisa said through gritted teeth. She pulled back the sleeve of her blouse and revealed a large black bruise that covered her entire shoulder. "He needs to recover."

Crowley's face flushed white. "What happened?"

"We went to this shady place looking for the missing kids and there were these tunnels underneath – Joucastle, that was the name of it. We went down there and there are dozens of these kids down there, Crow. *Dozens.* And they're all, well, fucked up. CPS has them now, but they were all good and fucked up. I have no idea what was being done to them down there – I can guess, but I'd rather not think about it."

Crowley nodded slowly.

"Xander went down but the leader, this fucking blonde bitch we saw in the videos… she's not normal. She's like Xander, not just like him, but you know, special. Different."

Crowley nodded, her head barely moving.

"Duncan shot her in the face and it barely slowed her down. It bruised her, but that was it. And she… she just *took Xander apart.* He's resting at Tim's and he should be fine, but… Jesus Crowley, you're glad you weren't there. I don't think I can unsee some of that shit."

Crowley nodded again, then brought her arms around Lisa and hugged her tight to her breast, feeling the warmth of her.

◆

"This situation needs to be dealt with and it's not being dealt with," Haybrook said, his voice haggard but authoritative.

The rest of the board nodded solemnly.

"Arthur has done wonders for this company since he got it from his father, but this – this is of a different magnitude. This is espionage by way of murder, I'm sure of it, and I will not stand by for it."

Again, nods from the Shane Board.

"I have No Confidence, and motion as such."

There was a sharp sound, like a fire alarm going off, something on such a high register that it made their ears sting.

There was the sound of a door closing, and Haybrook turned, expecting to see Arthur or Erica standing there, angry and shocked as anyone who overheard themselves being talked about was.

There was a tall, gruff man with piercing eyes that were tinged with pink sclera standing in the doorway. He had one hand on the knob still, and the other on a long blade which he held at his leg. He locked the door behind him.

They tried to run, but there was nowhere to run.

Duncan stood next to the ruined door of the Homicide12 holding cell, staring down at it with his hands on his hips.

"What could do this?" Janet asked, seeing the way the hinge bent back. "A ram sure, but how did someone get a ram past security?"

"I can think of a few things that could do this," Duncan said low and to himself, thinking back to the way his shot had barely fazed Celena and shuddering.

His phone rang, and he picked it up, looked at the caller ID, then answered. "Taggart, whatcha got?" He paused, listening. Janet turned to look at him, but he turned away. "White, slow down. The Board did what? Happened when?" His cheeks grew flush. "What did you just say?"

EPILOGUE

Xander cringed as he put his leg through the entrance to his apartment, and he felt something ache and pop in his kneecap. He had been on Tim's couch for a full three days, and Tim had tried to tell him that he needed more time there to heal, but Xander had insisted on leaving. Too much had happened since he'd been placed there, and he had to go back out and get into the thick of it, he'd said.

"Crowley?" he called, his voice gravelly and sounding strange even to him after days of not using it. His windpipe had been badly damaged in his fight with Celena, and was only now to a point where he could use it without intense pain.

There was no answer from the shadows of the house.

The toaster was not where it had been on the counter, nor was the coffeemaker. He stared at the empty voids where they had been for a moment, squinted, then stepped past the kitchen countertop and into the arch that led to the living room.

The Shane Board of Directors had been killed, the latest victims of the murderer that had been picking off members of their company one by one. Duncan had slept at Tim's two of the last three nights, pouring over the information on it. He'd come back from the autopsy report looking sickly, and Xander had tried to help.

The map was still on the floor of the living room, the Lego buildings he and Lisa had constructed to build their case still protruding from the paper and casting long shadows with the evening light.

"Lisa?" he called again, wincing as he turned his head back toward their bedroom and aggravated one of his bruises.

He opened the door to their bedroom.

Their beds were gone, as were all their belongings. Their closet was empty save for a few shirts that didn't look like they fit Lisa anymore, and there were clothes hangers strewn about over the floor in distressed clumps. They had begun to gather dust.

In the center of the room, near where Crowley's bed had been, was a single folded sheet of paper.

He walked over toward it slowly, his eyes trained on it as though he expected it to do something other than just sit there gathering dust in the vacant room. When he stood over it, he saw that his name was written on the back in the loopy, cursive handwriting that he recognized as Crowley's.

He pursed his lips, nodded once, then turned and left the room, shutting the door gently behind him.

AFTERWORD

This book went through a number of drafts. Despite being the fifteenth book published starring Xander Drew, I wrote its first draft fourth. This time between first draft and last was fully seventeen years. This version resembles the original only nominally.

I'm proud of this novel as it stands. I like it, I like what it has to say and the story it tells, and I hope you did as well.

I'd like to thank my editor Erin Vance for all her help on this text, and I'd like to apologize for the sleepless nights she endured after reading it.

This book is dedicated to my partner, Ellen Curtis, who makes me a better writer. Every day.

Matthew LeDrew
Nov 6, 2018
St. Johns, Newfoundland

ENGEN TIMELINE

With over twenty novels spread over three different series by many different authors, the Engen Universe of titles is growing every day and into genres we couldn't have imagined! From the original ten book *Black Womb* thriller series, its crime novel sequel series *Xander Drew*, our flagship adventure title *Infinity*, or single-novels like *Jacobi Street* or *light|dark,* there's something in the Engen Universe for everyone with more books by more authors on the way soon!

...But how do the events relate to one another, chronologically? While some astute readers have guessed at the potential timeline (some accurately, some not), we're going to finally set the question of the Engen Timeline to rest.

Turn the page for an up-to-date guide of the ever-widening world of Engen, featuring the works of Ellen Curtis, Andrea Hackett, Sarah Thompson, Jay Paulin, and Matthew LeDrew!

In the 10 Years Prior Black September

"Reptilia" by Matthew LeDrew
published in *light | dark*.
Danger descends on a small secluded town in the form of a deadly virus with fantastic and terrible side-effects. Can a small group of doctors escape alive?

Compendium by Ellen Curtis
Three short stories forming the basis for the Engen Universe's ties to suspense, genetic engeneering, and the supernatural. Features the stories "The Tourniquet Revival," "Falling into Fire" and "At Midnight, the Dawn."

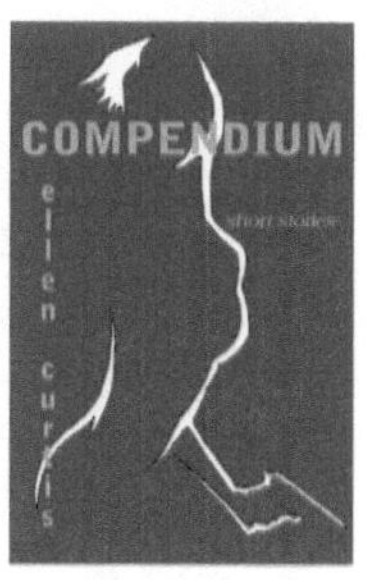

"The Theogony" by Matthew LeDrew
published in *light | dark*.
A tale of young Theo Flaherty of the *Infinity* series and his time admitted against his will to the Black Springs hospital, where he learns to paint, and seeks out his father.

Black September

"Revving Engen" by Matthew LeDrew
published in *light | dark*.
A direct lead-in to both *Infinity* and *Black Womb*, Tasha travels to Coral Beach, Maine on a hot tip about a recently discovered young man with incredible abilities.

Infinity by Ellen Curtis & Matthew LeDrew
Faced with a destiny he's uncertain of, the enigmatic Victor must bring together four unique people with very special abilities… or face the tasks ahead alone. Guaranteed to excite!

Black Womb by Matthew LeDrew
Fifteen years ago, something happened in Coral Beach, Maine that resulted in the present death of a seventeen-year-old boy. Now four high-school students must try to solve the mystery… before the killer picks them off.

Jacobi Street by Matthew LeDrew
When a mysterious painting shows up at an art gallery he works at, Bob must work with Eddie and Sloan to track down its sinister origins and convince the people living on Jacobi Street of them, before its too late!

Transformations in Pain by Matthew LeDrew
When two girls are assaulted and one is hospitalized, the residents of Coral Beach must put their shared tragedies behind them and stop the man responsible, as well as unlock the secrets behind the true nature of the Womb…

Year One: October

Smoke and Mirrors by Matthew LeDrew
The approaching trial of Genblade brings
closure to the people of Coral Beach, until
people start showing up dead in the same
manner they did when he was at large.

"Scarlett" by Andrea Hackett
published in *light | dark*.
Introducing Scarlett, the slightly damaged
hunter on a mission to save others from the
monsters from her past.

The Tourniquet Reprisal by Curtis & LeDrew
A man lives in Atlanta, Georgia that people
don't talk about, but everyone knows he's
there. He arrived a year ago and turned a
gaggle of uneducated youth into something
new, something to fear.

Roulette by Matthew LeDrew
As the teen suicide rate in Coral Beach starts
to climb astronomically fast, Xander travels
to Los Angeles to fight his most terrifying
adversary yet… and learns that the only thing
worse than looking for release… is finding it.

Year One: November

Exodus of Angels by Curtis & LeDrew
Victor's enigmatic past is illuminated when
Jaycee accompanies him to visit a new friend
in the paliative care ward of the Black Springs
hospital, where Theo also happens to be
searching for a cure for Leigh.

Ghosts of the Past by Matthew LeDrew
Coral Beach faces its most awesome threat
when one of Engen's past mistakes is
unleashed upon the unsuspecting populous.
Friends and enemies unite to fight a common
enemy… but will even that be enough?

Touch Your Nose by Matthew LeDrew
Simon Monk must infiltrate the San Fransico
branch of Shane Industries, a massive
company with deep ties to the Engen
Universe. Where do his true loyalties lie? And
can he get out without causing harm?

Ignorance is Bliss by Matthew LeDrew
After being set through the ringer one too
many times, Xander decides that his life with
Julie needs a little more attention… which is
bad news because a new villain has come to
town with his sights set on Adam Genblade.

"Gristle While You Work" by Jay Paulin
published in *light | dark*.
A short story centering around the rise of a
new, and possibly cannibalistic, serial killer in
the Engen Universe.

Becoming by Matthew LeDrew
For months Xander Drew has been doing his
level best to keep the streets of Coral Beach
clean, which means it's time for the forces of
darkness to strike back… all at once.

Inner Child by Matthew LeDrew
Julie is hospitalized with life-threatening
wounds to both body and soul. But the
real threat comes from the hospital walls
themselves, as a demonic presence makes itself
known to Xander and his friends.

End of Year One

Gang War by Matthew LeDrew
The Tees, a homicidal gang of evil men, has
finally been taken down by Xander Drew. But
his victory is short lived, as retired Tees are
mysteriously killed. With a town of suspects,
anyone can be the culprit… including one of
their own.

Chains by Matthew LeDrew
Sociopath Derek Smith has been freed from prison and is praying on the weak; and none are weaker than August Styles: a pregnant girl with Down Syndrome who has run away from home.

"Omega" by Ellen Curtis
published in *light|dark*.
A sinister division of Engen begins a series of experiments on pregnant women in a fashion eerily similar to those that created the original Black Womb project.

The Long Road by Matthew LeDrew
Xander meets the American people — and realizes that the world is harsh and wicked, but can also be soft and gentle, even loving. Xander Drew comes of age on the road, and sets his new direction.

Year Two

Cinders by Matthew LeDrew
Detective Horton enters a violent and dangerous world he didn't know existed beneath the veneer of order and structure that he has based his entire deductive method around.

Sinister Intent by Matthew LeDrew
One of the killers Detective Horton could not catch has resurfaced: a serial killer who flaunts his sinister intent in front of the Los Angeles Police Department, making it so that no one is safe.

Faith by Matthew LeDrew
Xander's mysterious and troublesome past returns to haunt him on the streets of Los Angeles; a place where even more people can get caught in the crossfire of the games of death and deceit that makes up his life.

Flickers in the Night by Matthew LeDrew
Lisa Rowdan is hunted by her haunting --
and powerful -- ex-boyfriend Ryan through a lonely city street. Can she escape him?
One of over twenty great sprine-tingling short stories!

Family Values by Matthew LeDrew
Detective Horton enters a violent and dangerous world he didn't know existed beneath the veneer of order and structure that he has based his entire deductive method around.

The Future

"Remers" by Sarah Thompson
published in *light | dark*.
In the not-too-distant future of the Engen
Universe, young athletes are the targets of a
scouting program to create the next stage of
super soldier with cybernetic enhancements.

THE XANDER DREW SERIES

Prologue: The Long Road (May 2014)

Book One: Cinders (April 2015)
Book Two: Sinister Intent (November 2015)
Book Thee: Faith (December 2017)
Book Four: Family Values (December 2018)
Book Five: Fate's Shadow (forthcoming)

COMING SOON FROM ENGEN BOOKS:

FATE'S SHADOW

A violent past case is reopened as Xander must contend with
Detective Thomas Horton, the vigilante Shadow Flame, and
a returning figure from his youth in Coral Beach -- all while
trying to prevent a murderer from running free. Can Xander
stay the course even as his world crashes in around him?

The early years of **Xander Drew** as he struggles with the evils of his small rural hometown of Coral Beach, Maine. Cursed with the heart of the Womb and the gift of seeing the world around him for what it really is, Xander must learn the hard lessons about the nature of humanity to traverse the minefield of criminals, gangs, and abusers that stand between him and ultimate happiness -- but most of all that **sometimes it takes a monster, to catch a monster.**

"THE WRITING OF ITS GENERATION- - VISUAL, TO-THE-POINT AND IN-THE-MOMENT."
- *The Northeast Avalon Times*

The Coral Beach Casefiles series by Matthew LeDrew:

Book One: Black Womb (October 2007)
Book Two: Transformations in Pain (April 2008)
Book Three: Smoke and Mirrors (February 2009)
Book Four: Roulette (October 2009)
Book Five: Ghosts of the Past (April 2010)
Book Six: Ignorance is Bliss (October 2010)
Book Seven: Becoming (April 2011)
Book Eight: Inner Child (November 2011)
Book Nine: Gang War (April 2012)
Book Ten: Chains (April 2013)

Epilogue: The Long Road (May 2014)

For more information, please visit

www.engenbooks.com

infinity

The world is changing, and we have to change with it. That was the one thing that Victor was really sure of when he started looking for special people: people who could change the possibilities of the future from something certainly grim... to something *infinitely* positive.

Now four unsuspecting people from different backgrounds and walks of life have been thrown into the mix together, and nothing will ever be the same. But there's a difference between hoping for a better world and actually having one, and there will always be resistance to change.

Book One: Infinity (October 2010)
Book Two: The Tourniquet Reprisal (October 2012)
Book Three: Exodus of Angels (April 2016)

Related Books:

       Compendium (October 2009)
       light|dark (April 2012)
       Roulette (October 2009)
       The Long Road (May 2014)
       Touch Your Nose (May 2018)

Written by the superstar author team of Ellen Curtis (*Compendium*) and Matthew LeDrew (the *Xander Drew* series).

Destiny doesn't wait for anyone.

ABOUT THE AUTHOR

Matthew LeDrew holds an Honours Degree in English from the Memorial University of Newfoundland with a minor in Anthropology, and studied Journalism at College of the North Atlantic in Stephenville, Newfoundland. He was honoured to be a jury member of the 2018 NLBA awards.

He has written nineteen other novels for Engen Books: the ten book Coral Beach Casefiles series, *The Long Road*, *Cinders*, *Sinister Intent*, *Faith*, *Jacobi Street*, *Touch Your Nose*, *Infinity*, *The Tourniquet Reprisal*, and *Exodus of Angels* the latter three of which with co-author Ellen Curtis.

He lives in St. John's, Newfoundland.

www.ingramcontent.com/pod-product-compliance
Lightning Source LLC
Chambersburg PA
CBHW020916060726
47591CB00004B/1278